# the memory cage

Ruth Eastham was born in Lancashire, England, and trained as a teacher in Cambridge. She has since worked in more than a dozen different schools in the UK, New Zealand, Australia and Italy. She likes photography, second-hand shops and world maps. Currently she lives in an international college with 26 teenagers from 23 different countries just down the corridor.

To find out more about Ruth, and receive free study guides for *The Memory Cage*, visit her website at: www.rutheastham.com

# the memory cage

## RUTH EASTHAM

■SCHOLASTIC

First published in the UK in 2011 by Scholastic Children's Books
An imprint of Scholastic Ltd
Euston House, 24 Eversholt Street
London, NW1 1DB, UK
Registered office: Westfield Road, Southam, Warwickshire, CV47 0RA
SCHOLASTIC and associated logos are trademarks and/or registered
trademarks of Scholastic Inc.

ISBN 978 1407 12052 2

Printed in the UK by CPI Bookmarque, Croydon, Surrey.
Papers used by Scholastic Children's Books are made from wood grown in
sustainable forests.

1 3 5 7 9 10 8 6 4 2

www.scholastic.co.uk/zone

For Mum and Dad

I tell this story so it won't be lost. The only sure way to remember things is to write them down. Grandad's illness taught me that. You need to remember things. Keep your secrets safe. And every family has secrets. Mine more than most.

What's your earliest memory?

Mine's with Grandad. On the beach near our house, collecting fossils.

I was seven, and that's the first picture of me in Mum and Dad's album. Before then, I didn't exist.

That's the way I like it.

No memories.

No me.

# PART 1

# THE PROMISE

# 1

# Trying To Put It Out of My Mind

*Breakfast table. Summer holidays, church fête Saturday. Chaos.*

**M**e trying to stay well out of it. Anyway, I had more important things to worry about.

I slid a bowl across the table towards Grandad. I couldn't help thinking, if he could just shove some cornflakes down him without anybody saying anything, then maybe we were in the clear. Maybe we'd got away with it.

I stretched over for the cereal packet. . .

"Let me taste more jam, Mummy! Let me!" My little sister, Sophie, tugged at Mum's elbow, fairy-princess wings flapping.

"Don't you dare get any on your costume!" Mum wagged the pen she was using to label jars. "Oh, of all the Saturdays to have to go into work, Richard! You'll be wearing yourself out with all this overtime!"

"Think I want to go in, Hilary?" Dad said. "And I might be a few years older than you, dear, but I'm not past it yet!" He lifted his *Financial Times* in front of his face.

I tipped cornflakes into Grandad's bowl. So far so good.

Sophie scooped leftover strawberry jam into her mouth from a saucepan, adding an extra layer to her smeared face paint.

"Greedy pig!" Leonard grabbed the pan off her. "Give it."

Sophie stuck her tongue out at him and started cutting up one of Mum's cooking magazines with a pair of pink scissors.

I splashed milk over my cornflakes, and then eased the milk jug towards Grandad.

"We should all be doing our bit for charity, Richard," said Mum.

"Yes, Hilary."

Leonard mouthed at me across the table. I knew he wouldn't miss a glowing opportunity like that. "Charity Case."

*Charity Case*. That's what he calls me when Mum and Dad aren't listening. Or his really witty favourite, *Bosnia Boy*. I wouldn't exactly say I got on with my big brother. You'd think things would be OK after six years. But I don't think Leonard ever liked the idea of me in his family. There was a lot more than just four months between us.

Grandad poured milk on his cornflakes. Some splashed up and dribbled down the side of the bowl.

I pushed the sugar his way.

He picked up his spoon.

Sophie picked up a glue pen and started sticking jagged-edged pictures of perfect cakes and summer salads on to the pages of her scrapbook.

"Remember your lunches!" Mum waved a hand over the row of boxes laid out across the middle of the table – Dad's white plastic one for the office, Sophie's pink glittery thing with fairies, Victoria's with its *East Kent Girls' College* emblem, Leonard's coffin-shaped one with the guns. My and Grandad's rolls wrapped in foil and stuck in a plastic bag.

"Crammed with healthy muck, no doubt!" said Grandad, giving me a wink.

"You've those photos still to get ready, William," Mum snapped back at him. "The fête starts at ten, remember!"

"Sugar, Grandad?" I prompted, plunging my spoon into my bowl and crunching in his direction. I felt myself sweating.

"I'm not carrying a lunchbox round!" Leonard stabbed the butter knife at his toast. "This is the 1990s, Mum, not the 1940s! I'll want a burger."

"Me too! Me too!" Sophie skipped around the kitchen with her scissors while Mum tried to get them off her. "With lots of onions and lots and lots of ketchup!"

For once, I agreed with Leonard, but I shovelled in more cornflakes and kept my mouth shut. Leonard didn't like me agreeing with him.

"Ketchup!" Sophie sang. "Ketchup! Ketchup! Ketchup! Who'll play with me now? Who'll play cocodriles and transhlers?"

"It's crocodiles and tarantulas, stupid," Leonard said. "Alex will."

"Who'll play cocodriles and transhlers?" Sophie wittered on. "Who'll come up with me to the secret room?"

"You stay away from that room, Sophie!" barked Dad.

Sophie had a thing at the moment for the room at the very top of our house. It was an attic room that nobody could get into and that Sophie thought was full of scary animals. Mum said it was far too dangerous because the floorboards were loose, and anyway, the lock was changed years ago and then the key was lost. Whenever I asked him about it, Grandad always changed the subject.

I looked over at Grandad as he sprinkled sugar over his flakes. His eyes had a faraway look and his spoon stayed hovering in mid-air.

*Eat*, I willed him. *Take a bite, for God's sake!* It was impossible some mornings, getting him to eat. But if I didn't try, who else would?

I wondered if he'd forgotten about last night. I sipped milk from my spoon and glanced around the table. Nobody had said anything yet. But I could have kicked myself. If only I'd kept a better eye on things. If only I'd watched him more closely.

Had we got away with it? I sneaked a look at Dad. Or was he planning to spring a surprise announcement when he'd downed the last of his coffee?

Bread popped out of the toaster with a clatter, smoking.

The smell made me feel sick. Leonard juggled a slice on to his plate.

The smoke alarm wailed out like a chisel to the skull. Mum flung open the back patio door and then snatched Dad's paper out of his hands and started fanning the detector with it. Shame the detector upstairs didn't do that last night. Then again, thank God it didn't. The din stopped.

Dad stood up with his coffee cup, scraping his chair against the wooden floorboards. The noise set my teeth on edge even more than the alarm. He looked really annoyed. Was this his moment to say something? I held my breath.

Dad took back his paper, then kissed Mum's cheek. "Be good, all of you." He disappeared out of the kitchen and I heard the front door slam.

I let out a long sigh of relief.

"Well done, Leonard," said Victoria, coming into the kitchen and eyeing his burnt toast. "Keep doing your bit for the greenhouse effect."

That's my big sister for you. Always going on at us about the environment. Conveniently forgetting about the telly in her bedroom and the fact that she drives to college, rather than get the bus. I wondered whether reaching seventeen did something to your brain cells.

Leonard sucked butter off his fingers, giving Victoria the evils.

Grandad sucked at his spoon.

I let out a snigger of relief and Leonard gave *me* the evils.

9

Grandad gazed out of the window, spoon grasped in his hand, his cornflakes turning to mush. I groaned to myself.

It was as if he'd never seen our back garden before, the long, moss-free lawn, the wicker garden furniture arranged in a circle Grandad said the builders of Stonehenge would have envied. He was staring past the Den, his big work shed with its curtained windows, down to the weeping willows and our old rowing boat, *Little Swift*, hauled out on the riverbank. I watched a look of confusion glaze his face. All of a sudden he sprang up from his chair and went over to the patio door, his fingertips pressed hard against the glass.

I chewed my cornflakes.

I knew Grandad was getting worse.

It had started small. Lost keys. Not knowing where he put his glasses. Lights left on. A window gaping open, the front door unlocked. Then breaking a glass and leaving the pieces lying there, eggs boiling dry so the pan got scorched. Then last night. . .

I felt cornflakes scrape the inside of my throat.

I covered up for him. Found his lost keys, his glasses, turned off lights, closed the windows, bolted the door, got rid of the glass, switched off the gas. Watched him whenever I could. But last night was different. That was the worst thing he's ever done. Setting fire to your pillow is not good at the best of times. Especially not good when the smoke detector on the upstairs landing's on the blink and you live in a big thatched house with Tudor timbering.

The phone started its irritating ringing. Victoria sighed – it was always for her. "Not another call!" She stood with a hand on her hip. "Hi. . . Five to ten. . . By the memorial."

I looked at Mum, then back at Victoria. You could see where my sister got it from. Her looks too – blonde hair, blue eyes, like Mum and Sophie. Leonard's the spitting image of Dad, especially when he scowls.

Me? You can't test family resemblances out on me.

Grandad was still staring out of the window, his profile grim. Who was he like? None of them. He was an outsider. Like me.

I saw his jaw twitch. "He's there again," he said.

"Is it Moggy, Grandad?" asked Sophie with interest, scrambling over to the window. "Oh, yes," she cooed. "There he is! We should stop putting so much milk down for him, Grandad. He's getting fat!"

At first I thought Grandad was joking with Sophie when he mentioned Moggy. But that was before I found him in the garden in his pyjamas, calling the cat's name over and over.

"Not ruddy Moggy," said Grandad with irritation. "That man. The one that's watching me. I told you. Don't you remember?"

"Sit down and get your tea, William." Mum pushed a mug in his direction.

I looked out. There was no one I could see.

Sophie started meowing at the top of her voice.

"Boyfriend again?" Leonard fluttered his eyelashes at

Victoria, who had just hung up.

"Grow up!" she hissed.

"*Three blind mice,*" sang Sophie. "*See how they run. . .*"

"Martin Dawes," pouted Leonard. "Oh, Mar-*tin!*"

"Mind your own business, Toerag!" Victoria screeched, storming from the room and stomping upstairs.

"*Twinkle, twinkle, little star!*" squawked Sophie.

I sank my head into my hands.

"Knock it off, can't you?" Grandad turned, leaving ten oily fingerprints on the glass, and there was a patch where his breath had been, fading to nothing. I looked at the soggy mess in Grandad's bowl and let out a long, quiet sigh.

"Come on, Sophie, darling. Finish your breakfast." Mum clanked jars of jam into a canvas bag. "You and I are leaving for the fête very soon. If we're quick we might see Lia there."

Leonard turned to me. "Yeah, Alex, how is that girlfriend of yours?"

I didn't even bother telling him for the three-millionth time that Lia Barker wasn't my girlfriend, she was a mate from my class. Not that he'd know anything about having friends.

Sophie started a full-blown shriek, making lethal swipes with her wand and losing a sequinned shoe. "*London's burning, London's burning, fetch the engines, fetch the engines. . .*"

"*Fire, fire, fire, fire,*" Leonard sang as he went by me on his way to the door. He brought his face right up to mine and said, all quiet, so only I could hear, "Don't think I don't know about last night."

My jaw dropped.

"Wait till I tell Dad. What will you do then, *Bosnia Boy*?" He pinched my arm hard between his fingers and I tried to elbow him away. "What'll you do when the loony van comes to take Grandad away? That'll teach you for trying to mess up our family."

I grabbed at his back, but he was already gone.

I gulped down my tea, trying to take in what Leonard had said. I watched Grandad strike a match, pipe in mouth. That stupid pipe of his.

"In the garden, William!" shrilled Mum. "How many more times? And remember we're counting on your photos."

He shook the flame out and looked at me. "Ready for the Den, Alex?"

I managed to nod back.

"You will watch Grandad, won't you, darling?" Mum whispered to me anxiously, pressing a tenner into my hand as we filed past. "Promise me."

I remembered last night. Waking up from a bad dream. Smelling smoke.

"Don't worry, Mum," I said, my heart thudding.

I'd got rid of the pillow. Buried it under the willows at the end of our garden.

We went out through the back patio door. The air smelt of grass cuttings and sunlight and the sea.

"Freedom!" Grandad lit his pipe and a fog of grey tobacco smoke rose and lingered over his head. "Feel like I've been let out of a ruddy cage!"

I kicked at the grass as we walked down the lawn. How had Leonard found out? I asked myself. He must have been sneaking about, spying. What if he told Dad? Would they send Grandad away? I knew for a fact that Mum and Dad had once discussed getting him on a waiting list for an old people's home. I also knew for a fact that Grandad would rather be dead than go in a place like that. But could they force him to go when they found out what he'd done?

I was sure about one thing. I had to talk to Leonard. Or Grandad was in big trouble.

We stopped outside the Den, Grandad finished his pipe, and I watched him unlock the padlock. As we went in, his toe caught on a saucer by the door, spilling milk all over.

"Ruddy Moggy!" he said with a grin.

Moggy. Grandad's cat. Not a problem in itself.

Trouble is, Moggy died fifty years ago.

# 2

## Grandad Makes Me Promise

*The Den. 8:30 a.m. A different kind of chaos.*

The door creaked open and we stepped into Grandad's darkroom.

It had a bench running along one side, with trays and bottles of chemicals for developing photos, and there was a large sink in the middle. At the far end was the door through to Grandad's Messing About Room. This wasn't your average garden shed.

I looked over at the photos for the fête, already hung along a string with small pegs.

"Your mum'll have my guts for garters if these blasted photographs aren't ready in time," Grandad said. "Let's get a move on, Alex!"

We worked in silence, taking the photos down, being careful not to bend them, putting them into see-through wallets with cardboard behind and a white card frame on top.

I'd always liked that about Grandad. The way we could

be in the same room for ages and not speak unless we wanted to. Grandad never tried to make me talk. Like about what happened to me. In Bosnia.

I sometimes get stuff coming back into my head and I can't stop it. I get bad dreams too. But I don't talk about them. I don't want to remember.

They tried to make me once. *Therapy*, they called it. Some man with a stupid tie and a big desk with neat piles of papers on it, and certificates in gold frames on the walls and an expensive leather settee.

It was like the time they tried to force me to go swimming. We were on the beach. They said they heard I was a good swimmer once. How I should have a go again.

But I never was a good swimmer. Not good enough. Not good enough to save my little brother, Nicu.

*You'll feel better if you talk about it*, they said.

I never did. I felt worse. It made them feel better maybe. I kept all that locked away. The stuff about my father, Babo. Mama. In the box under my bed.

Stupid Tie Man asked me about the swimming.

*"I'm not a good swimmer,"* I wanted to shout. *"A good swimmer would have kept hold of Nicu's hand."*

But I didn't. I told him a rude word instead. Jumped up and pulled a certificate off the wall and threw it on the floor and smashed the glass. Knocked over his piles of paper, and ran out.

Grandad laughed so much when I told him, I thought he'd die. Made me laugh too.

He understood. He always did.

Grandad never tried to make me talk.

Grandad wrote his signature across the frame of a photograph with his special fountain pen, then lifted it to his face to blow the ink dry. He passed it on to me to put inside a special plastic envelope.

It was good to have something to concentrate on. I tried not to think about anything else, except the photos, keeping them flat, stopping their edges curling under.

They were landscapes, the Kent countryside at the back of our house, places from our walks together. People in the village bought loads of them. The lighthouse overlooking the beach, the white cliffs, the grassy tracks along their tops. . . And there were his close-ups. A leaf caught on tree bark, the edge of a butterfly's wing, an ammonite fossil with its snail shell swirl.

I'd once asked Grandad why he never had people in his photos and he'd shrugged. He'd taken photographs of people during the Second World War, that was all I knew, but they'd got lost somehow. He never spoke about it. Said stuff like: "Some things are best forgotten."

*Yeah*, I told myself, *best forgotten*. Like last night.

"Right, that's those done." I listened to Grandad's rasping breaths and the clacking of the timer as he wound it up. "Just need to develop one or two more."

I thought we had plenty of photos to sell already, but I said nothing. Maybe Grandad was trying to impress Mum by doing a few extras. I supposed there was time.

"Remember to kill the light, Alex," said Grandad.

I remembered last night. How he'd nearly killed us all.

I pulled down the blinds, changing the room into darkness. Outside were the sounds of birdsong, the faint chugging of a tractor. I wondered again, did he even know what he'd done? Somehow, I couldn't bring myself to remind him. Maybe it was better he didn't remember. *Ignorance is bliss*, he liked to say. *Ignorance is bliss*.

I heard a switch click and Grandad was lit up red as he stooped over the bench. His lined face gave nothing away.

I used tongs to lay a fresh piece of printing paper in the developing tray and then Grandad tipped the tray, letting the liquid slide over the surface. I stared at his hands, at their criss-cross scars. I always wondered how they got there, but that was something else Grandad never spoke about. Something else he wanted to forget.

An image appeared in the tray, surfacing from the red skin of liquid like a memory coming back.

"Do you think they know, Alex?" Grandad said suddenly.

I froze. Pretended not to understand.

Grandad hung his head. I saw his hands tremble. His breathing came out in bursts, like little sobs. "I don't know what's happening to me, Alex."

I stood there. I wanted to put my arm round him, but it felt like stone.

Grandad rocked the tray so liquid splashed out on to the bench. "Why's an old fool like me staying where I'm not wanted. I know what they all think of me. Your dad hates my guts."

My voice was gravel. The words seemed nothing to what I felt. "*I* want you, Grandad."

Grandad held the tray still. "I know, lad. I know." He swatted at his forehead. "Whatever happens, I'll never forget *you*!" He said it as if it were a challenge to himself. An angry challenge. I heard his fear. I knew how to recognize fear.

"They'll put me in a ruddy home," he said. "For the virtually dead and buried. I don't want to leave this house, Alex. This house, well, it's. . ." I hardly caught what he said next. It came out in a kind of whisper. "This place is my life, Alex. Do you see? It's my life."

His voice grew louder. "It's got all my memories in it. . . It's where I lived with our Freda, your grandma. . . Where me and my brother Tommie grew up. . ." He put down the tray and gripped me.

"Promise me you'll not let them take me away." His hands were hurting my arm now. "Promise me."

He was so fierce, so sad. I wanted to cry out, but I couldn't. It was as if there was water in my mouth.

"I promise," I managed to splutter. "I promise."

Then Grandad was calm again, shifting the developing

tray like he was one of those blokes panning for specks of gold in a riverbed.

I stared miserably into the tray. How could I hope to keep a promise like that? Dad probably couldn't wait to get Grandad bundled off somewhere nice and caring and out-of-sight. If he found out what had happened last night. . . I couldn't cover up for Grandad for ever, could I?

Slowly, slowly, the image in the tray became clearer. It was a view of our back garden. There were Mum's wicker chairs in the foreground, an edge of perfect flower bed, the group of weeping willows beyond. . . That's where I thought I saw the figure, half-hidden between the tree trunks.

I was sure there was someone, standing there, watching, a staring, blurred face between the leaves . . . a figure all kind of hunched up. . . One shoulder looked lower than the other. It gave me the creeps, but before I could get a proper look, Grandad whipped the photo away and he was dipping it in the next tray and I was having to work the timer and check the temperatures of the chemicals, and then he was rinsing the photo under the tap and pegging it on the drying line at the far end of the darkroom. The paper quivered, dripping water on to the bench like spots of blood.

"Grandad. . ." I began. "Who. . ."

He tugged at a blackout blind and it swept upwards with a snap. The room was drowned in sunshine and for a few seconds I was blinded. I blinked hard. Dust hovered in the bars of light like flies. The memories of last night came buzzing into my head again and my question died in my throat.

Grandad thumped open a window. I smelt the sharp, salty smell of the sea. The church bell clanged. I looked at my watch. Quarter to ten.

"We'd better get going, Grandad."

He turned to me blankly for a second; then realization spread over his face. He picked up the pile of photographs. "Your mum'll be doing her nut."

I nodded, faking a grin. I followed him out, remembering to kill the red light on my way past. The safelight, it was called. But nothing felt safe any more.

# 3

# The Forbidden Word

*The church lawns. 9:55 a.m. Doing my nut.*

I knew I had to find Leonard. Fast.

I also knew Mum would kill me if Grandad's photographs weren't in on time. So we followed the sound of the brass band and the strings of multicoloured ribbons and dropped the photos off in one of the big white marquee tents pegged on to the church lawn. A notice over the entrance said "Art Sale" in dripping gold letters.

I waited while the Women's Institute woman counted them and set them out on a table. She was taking for ever.

"They're extremely good, Mr Smith, as always," she said. "We're most obliged to you."

"Call that art?" Grandad said loudly, peering at a painting of sheep hung on a display board. "*Kent Downs Flock*? More like ruddy dishcloths with legs!"

I smiled at the WI woman, who had paused in her work with a frown.

"You can't tell their heads from their backsides!" Grandad announced.

I decided it was time to get out of there. "Thank you very much," I said quickly to the woman, steering Grandad to the exit.

We joined the stream of people moving in the direction of the stalls. Now and again he would mumble something about being watched, but I was too busy looking out for Leonard to pay much attention. He had to be around here somewhere.

"Alex! Mr Smith!"

I saw Lia waving at us from behind her dad's stall, which was piled up with antiques. Suddenly I felt a bit better, seeing her.

"Got the vases your pa ordered," Lia's dad boomed, saluting me from behind a chamber pot. He was wearing a World War Two RAF uniform, a flying jacket, and goggles. "Tell him he can pick them up from the shop."

Lia came towards us in her wheelchair.

"Ophelia!" her dad sang after her. "Come back soon, my darling!"

"How embarrassing is that?" she said, rolling her eyes at her dad. "I told my father he looked ridiculous. Do you really have to dress up for the fête this year? I said to him. But does he ever listen to me?"

Grandad ambled over to Mr Barker's stall.

Lia tugged at my arm. "Hey, I found something you might be interested in, Alex. Over there."

She was heading off already and I had to run to keep up. As if I didn't have enough to deal with, finding Leonard. The trouble is, once Lia got an idea into her head, there was no stopping her.

"Here, Alex!" She pointed triumphantly at a table with a banner sellotaped across the front. It said *Raffle in Aid of Alzheimer's Awareness*.

I stopped dead. *Alzheimer's*. That's what Grandad had. We all knew it. The whole family. It was some terrible swear word we could never say. Like that other word. *Incurable*.

Grandad's words came crashing back into my mind.

*Promise me you'll not let them take me away.*

Lia must have seen the look on my face. She gave my arm a squeeze.

"It's OK," she said. "There's information and stuff. You can look and. . ."

I shrugged her off. Lia was always trying to get me to talk about things I didn't want to. I suddenly wished she'd leave me alone so I could get on with finding Leonard.

"Hello, Alex. Hello, Lia." Miss Kirby smiled up at us from behind the table.

I liked Miss Kirby. She worked in the village library, and would always help you out with school projects and stuff, but at that moment I was too uptight to be very friendly.

Her eyes flicked towards Mr Barker's stall, where Grandad was shaking his head at Mr Barker's RAF jacket.

"Get out your money, kids," she said. She leaned towards me. "If you buy a couple of my raffle tickets, Alex, I'll call it quits with the fine on your grandad's overdue library books."

I gave her a bit of a grin and fished around for some coins.

"That's what we're raising money for." Miss Kirby gestured at leaflets fanned out on the table. Lia took a couple and held one out to me. I handed over my money and took the leaflet with my ticket stubs, shoving everything into the back pocket of my jeans.

"Aren't you going to read it?" Lia sounded disappointed.

"Not now," I said.

"It has a telephone helpline and a website on the back," Lia went on. "You can. . ."

"Not now!"

Lia opened her mouth to speak, but just then Victoria appeared with Sophie, looking totally peeved.

"I always get landed with babysitting Sophie. It's not fair."

"Lia!" Sophie sprang up on to her lap. "Fast! Now!"

I looked over at Grandad. He was laughing, probably at some joke Lia's dad had told. You could hear Mr Barker's rumbling laugh from where we were standing. Grandad's shoulders were hunched and his whole body was shaking, and I remember thinking how frail he looked right then, next to big Mr Barker, like he might fall over any minute. Laugh himself to death.

Suddenly I wanted to get back to him, to be next to him, to take hold of his arm. . .

I edged away from the Alzheimer's stall. Lia was talking loudly to Miss Kirby, with Sophie still on her knee and emptying out the margarine tub of raffle-ticket stubs. Victoria was nowhere to be seen.

I edged away some more.

"You two make a lovely couple," sneered a voice beside me.

Leonard's.

"You and Lia. Two freaks together."

I pulled Leonard round a screen of tarpaulin on a neighbouring stall and got right to the point. "You can't tell Dad about last night."

"Thought you'd come begging," said Leonard. "Grandad could have burnt the whole house down. The sooner he gets put away, the better."

"What are you so against Grandad for? What's he ever done to you?"

"Hey, I've got an idea." Leonard ignored my questions and rammed a pointed finger into my chest, smirking. "What if I say you did it?"

I pushed him away. "I'd never. . ."

"But what if I say it was you? What if I say you've been trying to get Grandad into trouble?"

I couldn't believe what he was saying. "Why would I want to do that?"

Leonard tapped me hard on the head with his palm.

"Who knows what goes on in that warped mind of yours. You can't help yourself, can you, Bosnia Boy? You're always trying to get attention. You know Grandad'll get blamed if anyone finds out, so you're not bothered. You're always trying to break our family up."

I felt a stab of anger. What was he on about?

He gave me a shove. "Maybe the old idiot did it. Maybe you did it. It's my word against yours. I'll say I saw you fiddling about with Grandad's pipe."

I wanted to punch him. But what if he did go running to tell Dad? My promise slammed about inside my head. I couldn't let Grandad get in trouble. Would he even remember what he'd done? I'd have to tell Dad Leonard was right. I'd have to say it was me.

Leonard patted my head. "Dad and Mum will probably send you away too. They've always regretted adopting you."

"They can't do that!" I said, panic pricking at me. Could they? I'd been theirs for six years. Course they couldn't. Could they?

"Better start packing, Charity Case."

"Look, Leonard," I said. "You know Grandad was smoking in bed and fell asleep. . ."

Leonard thumped me hard in the chest.

I stumbled back. "He's been doing dangerous stuff for months!" I gasped. "You know it's his mind. He's. . ."

"You're the one with mental problems, Bosnia Boy!" Leonard landed a vicious kick on my shins. "You know why they shot your Daddy Babo, don't you? Cos he was mental like you. You know why they shot your Mummy Mama? Cos she was too ugly to. . ."

I stood there, bent over, gaping at him. I felt my chest heave. The ground seemed to be tilting, like a boat going over.

Leonard stared hard at me, a flash of red across his cheeks.

"Loser," he grunted. "Don't come crawling to me for sympathy. Nobody asked me if I wanted to share the house with you. I've had to put up with it all these years, you trying to take my place. Six years! The truth is I don't give a toss about Grandad and I don't give a toss about you."

He let out an unhappy laugh. "Don't think you can get Grandad on your side. He's getting more and more brain-dead by the day."

I flung my fist forward, catching Leonard on the jaw. He staggered back, blood on his lip. He dabbed at his mouth and looked at the red on his fingertips as if he thought it was a funny joke.

"Well done, Bosnia Boy," he said, walking away from me, rubbing the blood between his fingers. "Good one. Just what I need to show Dad what's really in that psycho head of yours."

# 4

# Mind Games

*The church lawns. 10:25 a.m. Using mind over matter.*

I struggled to steady my breath. I thought of going after Leonard, trying to reason with him again, but I knew it was no good.

I lifted the tarpaulin a bit and looked back at Miss Kirby's stall. Lia was still talking to her. Sophie was still jumping about wildly on Lia's knee.

I stood, trying to block out what Leonard said. His words, like bullets, stuck inside me. I squeezed my eyes shut and imagined skin growing over the holes, little by little, stretching to hide the dark circles until it looked like nothing was wrong. The ground swayed a bit more, and then went still.

I walked back to the stall and pulled out the leaflet, more to try and forget about what had just happened with Leonard than anything else.

*"Alzheimer's Disease affects 700,000 people in the UK alone. . ."* said the heading.

I caught Miss Kirby's eye, but she said nothing.

I scanned the rest. There were lots of science bits I didn't get – *brain scans, nerve cell connections, tangles and plaques. . .*

*"Their memory loss can lead to confusion, fear or anger. . ."*

Then some other stuff about how you could spend time with someone with Alzheimer's, like listening to music together, or making a scrapbook, or looking at old photos, or keeping a diary, or going for walks, and a chunk at the end asking for donations for research.

"Come on, Ophelia, love!" Mr Barker boomed. "I'm sweating cobs here! Need you to hold the fort while I get my Victorian paraphernalia sorted."

"I told him not to call me that!" Lia muttered. "But does he ever listen to me?" She sighed. "Parents!"

I saw Grandad wandering off from Mr Barker's stall.

*Memory loss.*

If only Grandad's memory was better, I thought. If only he didn't forget things, he wouldn't keep doing dangerous stuff, and he'd seem normal again and Mum and Dad would see he was OK and then they wouldn't have to think so much about care homes and sending Grandad away.

I shoved the leaflet into the front pocket of my jeans and went back to Miss Kirby's stall.

"Get down now, Sophie," I said. I still couldn't see Victoria anywhere. She'd managed to get out of her little babysitting job nicely. "We've to go with Grandad."

"Want to stay here!" she demanded, hooking her arms around Lia's waist and losing her fairy tiara in the process.

Lia giggled. "I'll look after you for a bit, Sophie-kins. You can come on my daddy's stall with me, would you like that?"

Sophie clapped her hands with excitement.

"She'll be a pain," I said.

"Who isn't?" said Lia with a grin, already moving off. "Bye, Miss Kirby! See you later, in your grandad's Den, Alex. About five, right?"

I nodded. "If you get fed up with Sophie, my mum's on the tombola. You'll need to check when the fancy dress competition starts too."

"No problem."

I caught up with Grandad by the entrance to another white marquee with an open front and lots of people milling about. I latched on to his arm.

"Much too sour," snapped a familiar, high-pitched voice from inside.

"Look who's talking," Grandad muttered. He sidled into the tent and I got pulled in with him, right into the middle of jam judging.

The vicar, Reverend Posselthwaite, was there, writing on a clipboard while a large lady with a knobbly walking stick leaned over a table laid with glass jars and small silver spoons. From the sound of it, our Great-Aunt Mildred had nothing good to say about any of the entries.

But then she never had anything good to say about anything or anybody, especially not Grandad.

Great-Aunt Mildred had helped look after Dad when he was young. Sometimes we didn't see her for weeks on end and other times we couldn't get rid of her; she'd prattle on, criticizing whoever she could in the village. *Nosy Old Bat* was what Grandad called her. She wasn't even our real aunt, just some kind of family friend. Except there was nothing friendly about Great-Aunt Mildred.

"I don't mince my words," she was saying to Reverend Posselthwaite. "But then one has to be cruel to be kind, one does. Cruel to be kind."

"Patience of a saint, he must have," Grandad said, nodding at the vicar. A couple of people near us turned round.

"Let's go before she slags off Mum's jam," I said, trying to exert some pressure on his arm and guide him back the way we'd come. Great-Aunt Mildred hadn't seen us yet, and I wanted it to stay that way. I was dreading what Grandad might blurt out next.

But Grandad was giving me a confused look. "Mum's jam?"

I felt my throat go tight. Had he forgotten already? The chaos in our kitchen only a couple of hours before?

Grandad gave a laugh. "Course! You know me, my mind's like a sieve!"

But I could see that it bothered him. I tried not to look as if it bothered me too.

"Next we have the dried flower arrangements,"

announced the vicar cheerfully.

"At least she's qualified to judge that one," said Grandad, and even more people turned to look at him. "Takes one dried-up specimen to know one."

Great-Aunt Mildred and the vicar passed on to the next table and I took the chance to get us away.

It got more crowded around the stalls. People jostled. I kept a firm grip on Grandad.

"Get your raffle tickets here! A pound a strip!"

The sickly smell of candyfloss filled the air from a whirring machine.

"Guess the weight of the cake! Fifty pence a go!"

The thumping brass band music was giving me a headache. The smell of candyfloss was too strong, making me feel queasy.

"Face painting only two pounds!"

"Get lucky on the lucky dip!"

"Roll up for the Tin Can Alley!"

We seemed to be pushed along by the river of people, not able to control where we were going.

That's when I saw the guns.

There was a row of them, lined up along a low bench, attached to the surface with clumsy-looking chains. In front of them were pyramids of battered cans, and tatty targets, yellow, orange, red. Big red bullseyes peppered with bullet holes.

I stopped dead. My breathing sped up.

"Come on, Alex, have a go!" called a woman. One of

Sophie's nursery teachers, I think, in a bright pink dress. "It's all for a good cause."

A boy from the class below mine snatched a gun and aimed it, his elbows set hard on the table. Crack, crack, crack went the pellets. *Crack, crack, crack*.

I felt myself start to sweat. Memories swirled inside my head, like sharks coming up from dark water.

"Have a go, Alex."

I backed away.

Kids came up from barrels of water gasping for air, their faces dripping and apples shoved in their mouths like pigs on a platter.

"Come on, Alex!"

I stumbled on the cans and crushed plastic cups that littered the ground, the paper cones with squashed remains of strawberries and cream. There were too many people. All pushing. Too much noise.

I felt a firm hold on my shoulders. Heard Grandad's gruff voice. "He'd much rather not, if you don't mind, miss. Not guns."

I saw the woman put a hand to her face and flush the colour of her dress. "Oh, of course. I wasn't thinking. I'm so sorry."

It suddenly felt like old times. Grandad looking out for me. Grandad himself again. My grandad. I felt the panic ebb away. I felt a surge of hope. I looked at him, but he strode on.

We passed the tombola with its display of prizes, wine, chocolates and bubble bath, but Mum was too busy collecting money and watching people pulling out corks from an old beer barrel to notice us.

We came across a stall that had a tray filled with sand, bits of matchsticks poking out all over.

"It's a memory game," explained the woman. "The hidden end of each matchstick is painted a colour. You have to pull out three of the same colour to win. Have a go?"

Grandad sniffed, not meeting my eye. "Looks a bit boring, this one, Alex."

Normally I might have agreed with him, but I saw my chance to give Grandad's memory a bit of exercise. If I was going to help him remember things, I had to start somewhere.

"No, you're right," I said. "You'd be rubbish at that one anyway," I teased.

Grandad took the bait. "Steady on, Alex. Steady on." He fished around in his pocket for some money. "I might just have a go," he said, giving the woman a pound coin and flexing his fingers.

I smiled. Was he trying to prove a point now, or what?

"But Grandad. . ." I protested with fake alarm. I badly wanted him to do well on the game. But then I realized, what if he didn't? The last thing I wanted was his confidence to get knocked.

"Maximum of seven tries," the woman on the stall said.

Grandad stroked his beard and then eased out the first matchstick.

"Yellow," he said, then pressed it back into the sand and

pulled up another. "Red. . . Orange. . . Green. . . Pink. . . Red. . . Blast it! Green!"

"Oh, hard luck! Well tried!" said the woman.

Grandad grunted and slapped another pound coin on to the table and the woman pulled a new tray all ready to go from under the table.

"Grandad. . ." I began.

"Let me concentrate," answered Grandad grumpily. "Let me concentrate."

He waggled out another matchstick. "Pink. . . Blue. . . Green. . . Black. . . Red. . . Red. . . Here we go! Here we go. . . Red! Hey, hey!" Grandad raised his arms in the air and did a little dance. "Who says the old codger's past it?" He bowed at the woman, then flapped his winnings at me. "Look at that, Alex. A crispy tenner. Hungry? I could eat a ruddy carthorse!"

I laughed with him. Lucky, Grandad, I thought. Very lucky. But he was happy, so what did it matter if the game had been a bit of a fluke? It proved something. When Grandad remembered, he was happier. If Grandad was happier, he was easier to get on with. Stopping him forgetting, I was convinced of it now, that was what I had to focus on if I were to keep my promise.

We moved away from the crowds to a patch of lawn by the church railings.

I took out the plastic bag with the foil-wrapped rolls Mum had made for us.

"Yes, Alex. Give those here."

Grandad took the bag from me, opened it, sniffed its contents, twirled it round in the air a couple of times, and then flung it into a nearby bin. He stood enjoying the shocked expression on my face.

"What your mum doesn't know won't hurt her," he said, grinning. "I've nothing against our Hilary, but I ask you! Organic chickpea butties with alf-ruddy-falfa! Now for some proper summer holiday grub!"

We followed the railings to the side gate that led on to the lane, and walked up the drive of the Uniformed Officer pub. We ordered food from the bar, and then Grandad bought me a Coke crammed with ice, and a pint for himself. We sat out in the garden at a wooden table between the weeping-willow trees, away from everyone else, under the shade of a big umbrella.

Grandad gestured back in the direction of the fête with a scornful look. "Warm beer in a plastic cup! I ask you." He held his glass to the light and sighed. "Now that's more like it."

We watched the river slide past, a mottled swirl of greens and browns. A couple of swans glided by, followed by three grey cygnets. A fourth one struggled after them, getting left further and further behind.

Grandad sat back with his pint while I crunched on cubes of ice. "You and our Leonard seem to be having a bit of trouble getting on these days," he said.

I gulped an icy lump and stared at him. He raised an eyebrow at me.

"We've never got on," I muttered.

Grandad gazed at a tangle of willow branches. "I was lucky," he said. "Me and my brother Tommie really got on. Did I ever tell you that? There's nothing like it, Alex. Brothers really close. Looking out for each other." He leaned towards me. "Maybe try and make a bit more of an effort with him. Leonard doesn't have many friends."

I felt ashamed. Then angry again, remembering what Leonard had said to me.

"When we've asked him to do things with us, he always says no," I said. "He's not even my real brother."

Grandad looked hard at me so I felt even more ashamed. "I'm not your real grandad then, am I?" He gave me a slanted smile.

"I didn't mean. . . It's just. . . Well, why did Dad and Mum bother to adopt me in the first place? What was the point? It's not as if they can't have children."

Grandad took another sip of his beer and ran a hand across his beard. "It was a photograph started the idea off, Alex," he said. "I saw it in a newspaper. A boy, it was. A boy looking out through the bars at the end of a bed. Like he was in a cage or something."

He rolled the glass between his hands. "Got me thinking, that photo did. It was the eyes that did it. Seemed to be looking right at me, they were. I couldn't forget those eyes. Got to me, they did.

"Well, I showed the photo to your mum and dad and

then we heard about people adopting orphaned kids and we talked quite a bit about it, and they liked the idea, of helping and that. Very generous your mum is that way. Very keen to do the right thing."

Something inside me shivered. That one picture. Grandad's idea. One photograph changing everything.

"All I'm saying about you and your brother, Alex, is, well, someone's got to make the first move. Leonard's an awkward so-and-so, I'll give you that. Takes after your father on that one, and me, I shouldn't wonder. Make more effort with him, that's all I'm saying. Who knows, then he might do the same with you.

"Bad blood in a family. . ." He paused and stared out over the water and I saw his jaw go tight-looking. "Well, it's not good, Alex," he said. "Believe me."

What did he mean *bad blood*? Was there bad blood in our family? I was about to ask him but he pushed his pint glass towards me. "Ruddy Coke. What you need is a sip of real ale, my lad!"

The waitress arrived with our food. Buttered white bread slabs, crammed with steaming bacon. I realized how hungry I was. Mouth watering, I lifted a slice and attacked the insides with the ketchup bottle.

We ate in silence awhile, both trying to stuff as much of our bacon sandwiches down us as we could without choking. As my stomach got fuller, I felt myself relaxing. I let the patch of sun falling along my shoulders soothe me.

Grandad suddenly held his nose so his voice came out

all squeaky. "Enemy sighted! Three o'clock! Take immediate evasive action!"

We grabbed the remains of our sandwiches and scrambled under the pub table. I saw Grandad's chest heave with stifled laughter. I stuffed a fist in my mouth.

I looked up through the bench slats.

It was Mum. She had hold of Sophie's hand. So at least Lia had been rescued. The vicar's wife, Mrs Posselthwaite, was with them and they were sitting a few tables away, partly screened from us by the drooping branches of a weeping willow. I heard Mum's voice, raised a pitch, something that always happens when she's trying to sound important.

I was surprised to see that Sophie had a burger. It wasn't like Mum to let her have junk food. A strand of fried onion was hanging from Sophie's munching mouth and she had hold of a big plastic bottle of ketchup, but Mum was too busy chatting to Mrs Posselthwaite to have noticed.

"There'll be tears," whispered Grandad. "Mark my words."

There was something about the way Mum and Mrs Posselthwaite were talking that worried me. Something wasn't right. As far as I knew, Mum only ever spoke to the vicar's wife about the weather, gardens or recipes. This didn't seem like one of their usual topics. I crawled a bit closer. I made out the odd word.

"Getting worse. . ."

"Aggressive. . ."

I heard the farting sound of the ketchup bottle from where we were hiding, so it must have been a good old squeeze that Sophie had given it. Anyway, the next minute the vicar's wife had this huge red stain all down the sleeve of her frilly white blouse and Mum looked totally embarrassed and was dabbing at her arm with disintegrating pub serviettes, all apologetic.

"Poor girl," muttered Grandad. "So bothered about what everyone else thinks of her."

And then, just before the church bell struck one, Mum leapt up, pulling Sophie with her, saying, "Lord, the fancy dress! We'll be late!" I was sure I heard her say, "Yes, I've heard the Sunflower Care Home's very good."

It hit me. She'd been talking about Grandad. About his Alzheimer's. She and Dad must have got more serious about sending him away, and they didn't even know half of what he'd been up to.

I let what was left of my sandwich fall to the ground. I don't think Grandad noticed. He had a confused look, as if he were trying to remember how he got to be under a pub table.

I scrambled back and helped Grandad up. He hobbled to standing, rubbing his knees. Somewhere nearby a drum sounded, a dull thudding, getting closer. The fancy dress parade, snaking its way over the church lawns towards us.

Grandad stopped rubbing his knees and stared ahead, his face frozen into a look of anger. "It's *him* again!" he hissed. Before I had time to react, he pulled away from my

41

arm. His voice had a furious tremor in it. "Come out where we can see you! Coward!"

I scanned the screen of tree branches ahead of us. I couldn't see anyone. I tried to hold on to Grandad, but he broke away from me. "This time he's not going to skulk away from me like some sewer rat! You come back here! I've got proof you're hounding me, you hear?"

Children in fancy dress streamed down through the beer garden, giggling and waving, Mr Barker alongside belting on a huge bass drum.

I saw Grandad lean towards a knot of willow branches, finger pointed, jabbing the space between him and the leaves. I heard little snatches of his shouting over the booming drum.

"Judging me. . ."

I tried to get closer, but the parade of children was separating us like a river.

"Traitor."

A French onion seller with a felt-tipped moustache, a fairy princess with one wing missing. . .

"Murder. . ."

Through the gaps I saw Grandad plough through the mesh of weeping willow and out of sight.

I struggled to get to him. My brain felt like a drum, being bashed over and over. Thud, thud, thud. . . Somewhere overhead, there was a flood of balloons into the sky. Green, orange, red. . . Red, red, red. . .

A ghost with chains draped round its waist barred my

way, a Frankenstein's monster with a bolt through his neck, a cowboy with two guns raised. . .

"Alex! Alex! I won a rosette! I won a rosette!" And Sophie was pulling me round and round and round with her and Mum was saying, "Where's your grandad? Oh Alex, you *promised* me!"

I turned away from her, my head still thumping. I was sick of it. Sick of all of them. Sick of promises I had to keep, but couldn't. Sick of secrets.

I plunged into the twisting tree branches, letting them snake around me and get right into my eyes so I couldn't see a thing.

# 5

## Lest I Forget

I remember tree branches overhead where we're hiding. Spots of sunlight on me like hot patches of blood. I lie with my cheek to the ground, smelling wet earth. Smoke. Then I am running again, falling, running, dragging Nicu along with me, his little hand gripping mine. . . Their gunshots following us. . .

I sat down panting and felt the cool press of stone against my back, waiting for the pictures in my head to go. Bit by bit, they faded. Slowly my headache eased off.

Above me, leaves flapped in the wind like fish caught in a mesh of branches.

I looked around.

Somehow I'd ended up in the graveyard. A hidden corner of it, overgrown with brambles and rhododendron bushes. The last place on Earth I'd usually want to be. All those reminders of death. But at least it was quiet. Away from people. Away from promises.

My legs were scratched where twigs and thorns had spiked me. I rubbed a finger along the beaded lines of blood and inspected the red stain on my fingertip. *Bad blood*, I thought. *Bad blood*.

I dug a fist into the soil. Where was Grandad? I tried to pretend I didn't care, but an image of him floating face down in the river kept coming to me. And that word he'd shouted before he'd disappeared. *Murder*.

I squeezed my eyes shut. Let somebody else worry about him for a change, I told myself. I listened to the rustle of leaves overhead, to the cooing of pigeons. The watery image sank away.

I squinted at the patches of sunlight, at the jumble of gravestones between the beech trees. I started reading a few of the inscriptions.

TO DARLING GEOFFREY
SON, BROTHER, FATHER

There was one with a broken angel on top, a grave for a boy, only seven when he died, it said. I shuddered and read another.

**LEST WE FORGET**
**PRIVATE JACK BRIDGES**
**1922–1944**

Lots of the carvings started with the words *"Lest we forget"* in them. Loads of the men in the village had been killed during the war; we'd learnt about it at school.

Grandad had known a lot of them. I'd managed to squeeze some information out of him for my class project a couple of summers before. He told me that most of them had been wiped out in one day, on the beaches of Dunkirk. Then he'd clammed up and gone off to his Den. Like I said, Grandad never wanted to talk about those things.

I looked around, as if half-expecting to see him standing there.

Another gravestone caught my eye. It was at a funny angle, as if someone had tried to push it over. It stood like an old tooth loose in its socket, a ridge of thick grass sprouting around it, coils of black-green ivy snaking up its marble surface. Because of its angle, it cast a longer shadow than the other stones.

Maybe it was its weird angle that made it stand out, or that long shadow, or maybe it was something else. The little vase of red carnations at its base. Not the plastic efforts you saw at most old graves, but real flowers, fresh flowers, placed in water. Something else was weird.

I shifted closer. The gravestone definitely looked vandalized, as if someone had been at the lettering with a chisel. I knew that gravestones got ruined sometimes, smashed with sledgehammers. It happened last year to some by the church. Drunks or druggies did it, Leonard told me. But if some drunk person had wanted to destroy something, I wondered, why would they single this gravestone out and leave the others? I ran my fingers into the grooves of the lettering. This vandalism was specific, even careful, as if whoever it was had taken a lot of time over it. Individual letters had been singled out and chipped away. There was a rectangular groove where each should be, all the other letters left intact.

WINIFRED ALICE SMITH

Smith. Our surname. There were millions of us in the village.

WINIFRED ALICE SMITH
BORN 1922
DIED 13TH OF MAY 1941
LOST TO US BEFORE HER TIME
FOUND BY OUR CREATOR
KILLED BY ███ , NOW LIVING IN LIGHT
BELOVED WIFE OF
PRIVATE SAMUEL THOMAS SMITH
(1920–1940)
A██

*And?* The word looked like an "and", but surely it couldn't be. It was impossible to read the rest.

A pigeon clattered through the tree branches, making me jump.

That floating image of Grandad came back to me.

I thought again about what Leonard had said. The look on his face when he'd said it, the way he'd punched me. I

47

pulled a twig from the ground and snapped it and hacked at the soil with a splintered end. How long would he keep his mouth shut? How long would it be, anyway, before Grandad did something dangerous again? What if he accidentally hurt himself? What if one of us got hurt? Victoria? Sophie?

I felt something scrunch in the front pocket of my jeans. The Alzheimer's leaflet I'd got from Miss Kirby's stall. I could show it to Mum and Dad. Tell them a cure was bound to be just around the corner, what with all the research going on. And I could tell them everything that had happened. Explain my side of the story, before they got the Leonard version. We could do something to help Grandad, together. Dad would back me up, surely, when he heard what had been going on. He was my dad, after all, even if I was adopted. Grandad was his dad, even if they didn't get on. That meant something. Didn't it?

I pulled myself up.

That was it, then. I'd decided. Telling Mum and Dad was for the best.

So why did I feel like such a traitor?

I started to walk home, following a trodden grass path that weaved between the trees and the graves. Narrow tracks broke off in all directions. I glimpsed the church tower through the branches and headed that way, finally finding the wide dirt lane that led back to the church lawns.

The crowds from the fête had gone. Litter drifted over

the grass. My trainers crushed down on shards of glass. Torn wrapping paper scuttled in circles.

An old man was hunched up raking litter from the flower beds, a bit of rag wrapped round his fist. Mr Webb, who looked after the church grounds. He shuffled around pulling up weeds and trimming things and wearing an anorak that was way too big for him. He had these medals pinned to his chest, even when he was mowing lawns, and he was always talking to himself. The kids in my school all said Peter Webb was mad.

He glared at me as I went past, as if I were the one to blame for all the Coke cans in his carnations.

I kept a lookout for Grandad. But there was no sign of him anywhere. I walked faster. What had I been doing just sitting there for ages? I should have been trying to find him! I broke into a run and took the path along the river. Nothing. I sprinted on. The wind tugged at a plastic cup and sent it rolling over the bank into the water, where it was carried away.

Still no Grandad.

By the time I reached the bottom of our garden I was sweating and gasping. No sign of him at the Den. The patio doors were open. The kitchen was deserted, the ruins of breakfast and jam-making still strewn over the table.

I could hear the sounds of shooting and explosions coming from upstairs, Leonard playing war games on his computer.

I heard Dad cough in his study. He was home from

work, then. I went and stood in the long hallway between the slightly open door and the ticking grandfather clock to get myself together. I had the leaflet ready. I'd smoothed out its crumples. *It may as well be now*, I told myself. *Get it over with.*

I peeped through the crack. Dad was busy at his desk, sitting on his big leather chair with his back to me, head bent over piles of papers. I knew he hated being disturbed when he was working, so I stayed standing there a while longer, peering in and waiting for the right moment.

Along a shelf by his desk was the row of antique vases he collected. I saw a black-and-white photo propped up amongst them. I'd never noticed it before, but then I'd never really been inside Dad's study for years, not since I'd sent one of his precious vases flying and it had smashed to pieces. Since then, Dad's study had been pretty much out-of-bounds to everyone. It may as well have been the forbidden attic room.

It was a black-and-white wedding photo. I recognized the woman in the white dress from a photo by Grandad's bed. It was Grandma, and standing beside her was a much younger version of Grandad. The photo had *1940* written across the bottom of it in thick black ink.

The grandfather clock in the hall continued its dull, loud ticking.

I tightened my grip on the leaflet and decided that there would never be a good moment for what I wanted to talk to Dad about, so I may as well go for it.

As it happened, I never got the chance to say anything, because just then I heard Mum coming, calling for Dad in an agitated kind of way, her shoes clacking on the wood floor as she swept into the study from its other door.

"Richard! William's still not home. I've been all over the house!"

Dad gave a short, tense laugh. "He's probably sipping beer at the Uniformed Officer as we speak!"

Neither of them were bothering to keep their voices down.

"It's nothing to joke about, Richard. My nerves are shattered as it is."

"Did you ring around? Find out if anyone's seen him?"

I saw the worried look on Mum's face. "I thought it was best to keep this to ourselves. Until we've looked properly, I mean."

"Do you think I've got all day?" I heard Dad sigh. He sounded well irritated. I saw him pick up the phone and bang out a number.

"Yes, Officer Barnes, please. It's Richard Smith."

(PAUSE)

"I'm so sorry for the trouble, Jim. . . Yes, you guessed right. William."

(FALSE LAUGH)

"The likely thing is he's gone walkabout again, but, you know, Hilary's quite anxious."

(PAUSE)

"This afternoon. About one thirty. The beer garden at the Officer."

51

(ANOTHER FALSE LAUGH)

"Yes. That's what I told her! Yes. . . OK. . . We'll do that. . . Fine. . . Many thanks, then. . . Yes. Goodbye."

Dad put the phone down. "Silly fool!" he muttered.

Somehow I guessed he wasn't talking about Officer Barnes.

"We can't go on like this, Richard." Mum's voice started going higher. Always a bad sign. A very bad sign. "He's definitely getting worse. He gets aggressive too. His swearing has become terrible, and as for that old, smelly cardigan with patches on the elbows he insists on wearing. . ."

"Don't worry, Hilary." Dad leaned back in his chair. "The police are out looking for the cardigan as we speak and will arrest it on sight."

"Oh, Richard, stop it! Could you start taking this seriously for once!"

There was a pause, and then Dad's voice sounded strange, sort of too calm, as if he were trying to hold back loads of anger and it was hard for him to do it. "I take this very seriously, Hilary." He opened the drawer of his desk and started leafing through a book.

"We'll have to bring the date forward," he said quietly. "Matron said there might be an opening at the Sunflower."

I pressed myself against the wall. Felt the cold radiator dig into my back.

"What other choice is there?"

The Sunflower Care Home. Mum's conversation with the vicar's wife.

"Well," said Mum uncertainly. "There doesn't seem to be any other way, does there?"

"None whatsoever."

"He's in his eighties, after all. . ."

"It's what's best for him."

"It's further away, I know, but the facilities are marvellous. . ."

"He'll be well looked after."

So they'd decided then. That was it. They were going to send him away.

I know I should have tried to stop them. Shouted, *You can't do that! You can't do that to my grandad!* I should have jumped out from behind the door and told them how much I wanted him to stay. Pleaded with them. Promised to look after him. But I didn't.

"There's the children to consider, Hilary."

"Yes. It will be good for Alex, won't it?"

*Good for me?* What were they on about? They didn't know anything! I wanted to press my fingers into my ears, shut out their stupid talking, but I had to keep listening. Forced myself to.

"Alex and William live too much in each other's pockets as it is," said Dad.

I heard him pick up the phone again. There were the sounds of dialling.

"Yes." I imagined Mum's head nodding up and down,

up and down. "If Grandad, well, if he wasn't on the scene any more, it might give Alex a chance to get on better with Leonard, or make some other new friends besides Lia. After all. . ."

They didn't know anything! I hardly heard Dad's phone call to the Sunflower. I was too upset; too busy thinking, *If only I hadn't lost him earlier*. . .

"They can take him in a week. Saturday."

If only I hadn't lost him by the river.

"What? A week today? Next Saturday? That soon?"

"Yes, matron. Yes. Thank you. We'll bring him on Saturday afternoon."

But I'd lost him.

"We can't go back on our decision now, Hilary." Fingers drummed on the table. "They're keeping a place for him."

"Well, if he's not any better in a week. . ." I heard Mum say.

"Unlikely," Dad cut her off. "Let's face the truth. There's no cure for what he's got and there never will be. No, Hilary. The decision's made. His memory's getting worse and worse. It's a lost cause."

I heard Dad's leather chair squeal. "Now I've to go and find the old fool."

I wanted to scream at them, *He's not a lost cause! He's ill*. I wanted to shove the leaflet in their faces. *See this*? But I stayed there by the door like a coward.

One thing was clear to me now though. I couldn't expect

any help from them. In one week, Grandad would be gone. I felt my knees wobble.

One week.

I stumbled along the hallway. They were both too busy planning how to get rid of Grandad to notice me. If they could get rid of Grandad so easily, was I next?

I almost tripped on the rug as I scrambled to get out. That's when I came face to face with Grandad, and his huge black eye.

# 6

# White Feather

*In the kitchen. 4:45 p.m. Playing Happy Families.*

I didn't think then was quite the right time to ask Grandad why he'd been talking to a willow tree, and when I tried to find out later how he'd got hurt, he shrugged.

The swollen lips I'd given Leonard didn't look like much next to Grandad's eye. I just hoped he'd keep them shut.

Mum had opened the patio doors in the kitchen so we could eat outside, though Leonard complained it was too cold and that he wasn't hungry enough and sat by himself at the far end of the wicker table. Victoria was out, as usual.

Grandad let Mum fuss over him with ice packs and tinned salmon sandwiches with cucumber, and seemed oblivious to Sophie's tantrum over Dad not letting her have another chocolate biscuit and Leonard's sneering looks. He sat there with a tartan rug on his knees, staring down the garden.

The old Grandad would have said something like: *You should have seen how the other bloke came off*. But he didn't. He sat there as if he weren't seeing any of us. As if he were somewhere else entirely.

Just as well, I thought. Better to be out of it with what your beloved family have got planned for you.

*One week*. The thought shuddered through me. I felt like my ribcage was being squeezed, crushing all the air out of my lungs. If only there was a way to prove Dad wrong. To show him Grandad could get better, that he wasn't a lost cause, that he could remember things. If only there was a way.

I sat having to watch Leonard shovelling sandwiches into his mouth. I remembered what Grandad had said about making more effort with him. I decided to try, but not for the reasons I guessed Grandad had meant. I was thinking how it wouldn't be the best timing for Dad to hear about cremated pillows anytime soon.

I waited until Mum, Dad and Sophie had gone back into the kitchen.

"Want some?" I nudged the teapot towards Leonard. He ignored me.

"We could go on our bikes after this, if you want," I said. "Along the lane."

He looked up. "No good being all sugar sweet, Bosnia Boy," he hissed. "I'm still waiting for the right moment to tell." He jerked his head towards where Dad was peeling an apple as Sophie cried and stomped around him and

Mum opened more salmon. Grandad continued to gaze into the distance. "D'you think now might be a good time?"

I tried to look as if I couldn't care less, but I felt my hand shake a bit as I poured myself a tea.

Leonard went back to behaving like I didn't exist.

I pushed my sandwiches away and sipped my drink. I found it hard to swallow even that.

I saw that Grandad was looking at me now, but in a really strange way, like his eyes were searching my face for something. After a bit, the look passed and he gave me a wink. "Den time, I reckon, Alex, don't you? Isn't Lia supposed to be joining us?"

"Princess Lia Ophelia!" Leonard gave a scornful laugh. "That girlfriend of yours should start living at our house. She spends enough time here."

As if on cue, our side gate swung open.

"Lia's *here*! Lia's here!" chorused Sophie, instantly stopping crying, and clapping and bouncing about like her feet were on jelly. "Come and play cocodriles and transhlers with me, Lia. Come on! Mummy, I want to go in the locked attic room with Lia!"

"For the last time, Sophie. . ." started Dad.

Leonard muttered something nasty and slouched in.

"Hey," I said to Lia.

She must have seen there was something wrong from the look on my face, but then she must have seen Grandad's eye because her mouth fell open. I shot her a warning glance and she had the sense not to say anything. She gave me a questioning look, but I just shrugged and swigged down more of my tea, trying to stop my hand trembling in the process.

"Ready for the tracks, Lia, girl?" said Grandad.

"You bet!" said Lia. "But I can't stay too long, Mr Smith. I'm helping my dad in the shop later. I told him he treats me like a slave, but does he ever listen? If he paid me for all the work I do, I could be retired already, I tell you."

The three of us made our way down the garden, while Sophie raged at the window and Mum tried to pacify her with a chocolate biscuit.

As we went through Grandad's darkroom, I remembered the photograph Grandad had been so keen to hide earlier. The creepy, blurred face and the funny shoulders. I saw there was a single photo left pegged up on the drying line, its back to me. Could that be the one? I let Grandad and Lia go ahead, and then I quickly went over.

I twisted the photo round. There was nothing but cliffs and beach, the sea with a fishing boat. There was no sign of the other photo. So what had Grandad done with it? Why had he been so keen to hide it?

I went to the door at the far end and walked into Grandad's Messing About Room.

"Oh I love this place!" Lia was saying, spinning herself round in her chair, her eyes all lit up like a kid's. "I could live here all the time, for sure."

Grandad's Messing About Room was bigger than the

darkroom. In one corner there was a sofa, piled up with old pillows. Grandad used them for kneeling on when he was working on his train set.

Next to the sofa was a tall bookcase crammed with Grandad's biscuit tins of tea cards. Packets of tea used to have cards in them and you collected sets of all sorts: birds, cars, flags, you name it. Grandad had thousands of the things.

There was a cardboard box where we kept our fossil collection, and leaning up against it in pride of place was our ammonite, a fossil the size of a dinner plate with a snail shell pattern.

In another corner, sitting on a round table with lion's paw feet, was an old gramophone with its big metal funnel. A pile of records was stacked under the table.

There was a small sink, a fridge, a kettle and a cupboard for supplies. There was a tea chest with three rickety chairs clustered round it. But the most totally amazing thing in there was the train set.

Tracks weaved their way around the entire room. Single tracks, double tracks, bends and inclines and long straight runs. There were tunnels under roads and bridges over rivers, train sheds, sidings and signal boxes. There were houses made from matchsticks, and churches and sheep on hillsides, a tractor ploughing a field, a tinfoil lake with sailing boats and tiny plastic ducks.

There were platforms with tiny plastic people carrying tiny plastic suitcases, mothers wheeling babies, fathers in hats and suits, children waving on their way to school. People. Families. Scenes frozen in time.

There were trees and grassy fields leading to the tops of white cliffs. We'd used real sand to make the beach at the bottom of the cliffs, and we'd spent for ever using clear plastic bags and blue and green sweet wrappers to make the sea look the way we wanted it.

Grandad and I had created a whole world, right there in that room, and I loved it more than anyone. Hours we'd spent, Grandad and me, adding this detail and that, painting and repairing and nailing new track. I loved that room, but right then I felt too upset to appreciate it much.

Lia pulled me from my brooding. "Look and learn, Alex!"

Grandad handed her the control box, a square black thing with dials and buttons. An engine gathered speed around the track, sending out orange sparks, pulling its string of carriages. There was the familiar smell of hot metal.

"I've to watch you like a hawk, my girl," said Grandad, smiling. "You'll be beating my record if I let you in here too often!"

And Grandad was just like his old self. Cracking jokes, having Lia in stitches. It rubbed off on me. Soon I was screaming with laughter. I couldn't stop. I probably sounded demented. I guess it was a release of tension or something.

Lia had me in a headlock. I pushed her chair towards

the sofa and she grabbed at the pile of pillows. She slapped one down at me and I dodged her, took a pillow and got her on the shoulder. Pillow raised, she launched herself forward with a screech and landed a blow on the side of my head. Grandad roared with laughter. He had a pillow too and was swiping at us with it. There was a tearing sound and a white cloud whooshed upwards and there were feathers everywhere. Me and Lia started scooping up handfuls of them and throwing them into the air and pelting them at each other. . .

. . .I'm not sure what happened next, but one minute we were all in hysterics, then the next Grandad was screaming at us. He was shouting, angry, his face all red and his black eye even more puffy-looking so you couldn't see the eye at all. "Get out, the pair of you!"

Lia and I stopped to gape at him.

"I told you never to come in this room. Never! How did you get in here anyway, eh?" Grandad stood with his hands in fists and a wild look. His breath came out in stabbing bursts. I was scared, seeing him like that. "The key's lost, I tell you. You had no right. Get out, I said. Get out!"

"Come on, Alex." Lia nudged me towards the door with her chair.

I didn't move. I kept staring at Grandad. I felt Lia elbow me in the ribs. It must have hurt.

In a daze I let her guide me out until we were both back in the garden.

"Well, I wonder what all that was about." She blew at her fringe.

I shrugged. Didn't trust myself to speak. We were in the shade, but I felt my face burning.

Lia wheeled herself a bit closer to me. "Alex, your grandad. . ." She paused. I knew she was trying to think of something to make me feel better. "I don't think he can help it. What with . . . well . . . you know, the Alzheimer's."

I nodded, biting my lip.

Grandad reappeared, all apologetic smiles, gripping the door frame with his big, scarred hands. "It's nothing," he said, and I heard his voice shake. He tried to laugh it off. "Sorry, you two. No harm done." He slapped his palms and rubbed them together. "Hey, anyone fancy a Coke on the way to the fête, after I've finished off my photos?"

"The fête's finished, Mr Smith," said Lia gently. "I think you got your photos all done, didn't you? I heard they sold like hot cakes."

I nodded at Grandad, faking a smile.

He nodded back slowly. "I see. I see."

There was an awkward pause and then Lia said, "Well, I'd better be going to help my dad out now. He's had a delivery and needs to price things up."

Grandad nodded again. "Best go then, my girl. Don't keep your dad waiting."

"Thanks, Mr Smith!" Lia moved off, shouting back over her shoulder. "Thanks, Alex. See you tomorrow." She sighed. "Unless my dad comes up with loads of jobs for me to do in the shop."

"Nice girl, that Lia," said Grandad.

We watched her go, and then both seemed to find something extra interesting about the patch of Mum's moss-free lawn between our feet.

"Sorry, Alex," Grandad mumbled at last. "In front of your friend and all that. It's just. . ."

"What did you mean about us not being allowed in the room?" I asked him. "About the key being lost?"

Grandad looked away. "It was nothing, Alex. I. . ." He stared into the distance.

He'd meant the attic room, I told myself. He must have done. For a minute his mind must have been playing tricks on him and he'd thought we were in there. But why would that have upset him so much? Why would he never talk about that room? What was there inside it?

Grandad slapped my back. "Ready to help me get the photos for the fête done then?"

I paused, deciding whether to push him more, but he looked so miserable right then, with his bruised eye and his hunched shoulders, so confused, so lost, that I decided not to. I thumped his arm gently. "Course, Grandad."

But at the door of the Den he paused and turned to me, all afraid. "Do you think they know what I did, Alex?"

He was talking about nearly burning the house down, wasn't he? Or had he forgotten already? Had he forgotten what he'd made me promise?

I started to speak but then he said, "I need a walk. Fancy a walk?"

We walked in silence along the footpath that ran along the side of a field to the cliff tops. I wanted to reach out and touch his shoulder, tell him everything would be all right. But I knew it wouldn't be. I didn't believe in fairy stories. I gave up believing in those when I was seven.

Now and again, Grandad looked back over his shoulder. He got me doing it after a while.

The view spilt open in front of us. The slab of blue-grey sea, the white curve of the cliffs to either side. The special cove where we'd spent hours collecting our fossils. Dark clouds hovered over the water, covering the sun. The wind pulled at my hair and made my bare arms feel cold.

*They're putting him in a home. They're putting him in a home.*

We passed by a small concrete building sunk into the ground, with slits for windows facing the sea. There were more of them dotted along the path. They were lookout bunkers, *pillboxes*, Grandad had told me once, from the Second World War. People had used them to watch for enemy boats, or planes flying in. He'd told me there were hundreds of wrecks of planes and boats on the bottom of the Channel from the war. I stared down from the cliff and watched the tide lick at the grey sand.

A boy in my class had found a rusted hand grenade washed up on the beach a few summers ago. He'd wanted to bring it in to class, but our teacher had said no, she didn't care how safe his dad, who was ex-army, said it was.

Grandad sat down on top of the bunker. "Do you think they know what I did?" he said again. He turned to me. "I wanted to tell you a few things, Alex," he began. "About our family. About things that happened during the war, and after."

This was something important to him, I could feel it. Something very important, and it was difficult for him to find the words. He stared out to sea and pulled at his beard.

Seagulls circled overhead and he reached into his pocket and flung up a handful of bread scraps and they swooped and snapped for them.

"The memories are there, somewhere." He tapped his head. "Have to be, don't they? Somewhere."

He tossed up more crumbs and the seagulls squabbled and flapped over our heads. "I've just got to find them and stop them getting lost."

Grandad stood up and the seagulls screeched away.

"My mind's like the tide," he joked grimly. "It keeps coming and going, and I've no damn control over it."

I nodded at him and tried a smile.

Grandad sighed. "I'm afraid that the tide's out most of the time these days, Alex." He held up his hands towards the sea. "It's something like that King Canute bloke – you know the one? He commanded the tide not to come in." He gave a short laugh. "Maybe he'd built a sandcastle or something and didn't want it wrecking! Anyway, even old

Canute should have known that to try and stop the sea was a pretty daft thing to do."

I nodded again. I waited. We sat in silence. Grandad stared out at the sea some more.

I looked down at the beach. The wind had picked up and sand was being blown across it like smoke. Somebody had written something there. The letters were big enough to read from right up where we were. *Jo was here*. I watched the tide creeping in, the slow, dark spread of water starting to lap at the edges of the words.

The sea was like Grandad's Alzheimer's. Coming to wipe away everything that was written in someone's life. All the things they'd done. All the people they'd known. All the things they'd felt. Stealing away their memories.

What was somebody without their memories?

*William Smith was here*. I imagined water swirling over the letters, filling the troughs until the sides of the letters crumbled away and there was nothing left.

Grandad cleared his throat.

"My brother. . . Your grandma. . ."

I realized my fist was clenched and when I opened it there was something caught in the moist crease of the palm. A single white feather.

"During the war. . ."

He stopped. He stared at me. That look again. Only this time I realized what it was.

It came to me like a wasp sting. Worse. An axe in the head. A bullet.

He was staring at me with that ugly purple-red eye of his, as if he'd never seen me before.

My body went tense with shock.

He didn't know who I was.

Pain heaved through my chest. Grandad had promised he'd never forget me.

He'd promised.

His face changed again. Relaxed into a smile. But it was too late. I'd seen the way he'd looked at me, even if it was only for a few seconds.

He'd forgotten who I was once and it could happen again. What if next time he didn't ever remember me? Leonard's words shunted into my head. *He's getting more and more brain-dead by the day.*

That's when I knew I had to do something.

Right away. I just had to.

Before it was too late.

I led Grandad back along the cliff edge as the storm clouds moved in from the sea like enemy boats, and the grey tide turned on the beach far below.

Grandad promised he'd never forget me. The thought kept spiralling round in my head as we walked home. But how could I expect him to keep a promise like that?

It began raining. Cold drops speckled my T-shirt and I shivered. How could I ever hope to keep my promise either? How could I ever hope to stop Grandad forgetting?

We got to the village and passed the post office, the

village shop, the train station with a sign that said *Lost Property*. If only you could go in there, I thought, and get back lost memories instead of umbrellas. If only it were that easy.

The road continued alongside the tracks a while. My trainers splashed on the wet pavement and I thought about the tracks and houses and plastic families of Grandad's train set.

We got home. I left Grandad to go in by himself. I couldn't face it. Not right then. I heard voices as the door swung open. Smells of one of Mum's casseroles wafted out.

I heard Mum say, "William, you're soaked. You'll catch your death," and then, "Wasn't Alex with you?"

I crouched against the wall where there was a bit of shelter from the rain and pulled the damp collar of my T-shirt around my throat.

Water ran down the side of the house from a cracked gutter and splashed on to the ground. Little rivers of rainwater branched along the tarmac of the drive before swirling in dark pools where the drain was half clogged with mud and leaves.

*Alex*. A voice. From inside my head. Nicu?

*Help me, Alex.*

I gripped my knees and rocked myself.

Forward and back. Forward and back.

*Upomoć, Alex! Upomoć!*

I watched the water swirl and churn.

I stayed there, not wanting to go in. The thought of not

69

being able to do anything, of having to explain to Grandad that he was a lost cause, that I'd broken my promise to him and he was being sent away. . . Better not to think about that. Better not to.

I stood up. My knees were stiff from the cold and the crouching. I could see everyone in the lounge through our big bay window.

Victoria on the phone. Grandad sitting in his armchair with his feet up and a blanket over his legs. Mum and Dad and Leonard watching telly in a line. Sophie cutting up Dad's newspaper, scrubbing at the pieces with a glue pen and slapping them into her scrapbook.

I patted my jeans pocket and pulled out the crumpled Alzheimer's leaflet. It ripped as I tried to open it. It slipped out of my fingers and dropped into a puddle. I lifted out the soggy mess of words. . .

. . .*tangles . . . connections . . . memory loss . . . old photos . . . scrapbook. . .*

I looked up from the leaflet.

Gulls circled in the fading light.

Grandad's words came back to me.

*The memories are there, somewhere. . . Just got to find them. . . Stop them getting lost. . .*

An idea started forming in my head, a spark of hope.

Maybe there was a way to stop Grandad forgetting his life. Maybe there was still a chance to keep him with us and keep my promise.

I needed a real way to bring his memory back. Some

way to keep his memories alive for him and keep them safe. My heart pounded as my plan took shape.

I was going to make a scrapbook.

I would find out as much about Grandad's past as I could and put it in. I would write stuff and cut out stuff and stick in pictures and postcards and leaflets. Places he'd visited, people he knew. I would show Grandad the scrapbook. Keep reminding him of where he'd been and what he'd done.

Keep reminding him who he was.

I wasn't going to give up on him. I wasn't going to sit around and let things happen. I was going to do something!

Maybe I was desperate. I told you, I don't believe in fairy tales. But at that moment I really thought I could do it. I really thought I could change things. That I could still keep my promise. I had to believe it.

Had to.

And I had one week.

# PART 2

# A SCRAPBOOK OF MEMORIES

# 7

# Freda and Tommie

*In the Den. Losing track of time.*

Istarted with photographs.

Grandad and I sat in the Den and went through the family albums, one after the other.

At first there were pictures of things that I remembered too. Waving from the turret of Dover Castle. Mum pregnant with Sophie, resting a plate of chocolate biscuits on her belly. Rowing the *Little Swift* along the river.

There was the family holiday when Dad had slipped on a cowpat and fallen backwards into a hedge. We had a good laugh about that. There was a photo of us all sitting on a picnic rug in the garden, smiling at the camera, with me sandwiched between them, and I couldn't help thinking, They'd already got two kids, why'd they want *me*?

Grandad was a bit shaky on some of the details, but he soon got into the swing of it and, with a few reminders from me, he managed to come out with all these funny stories, even remembering things that I'd forgotten.

I'd told Mum that I was trying to cheer Grandad up and she had agreed that I could take pictures out of the albums, so long as I was careful with them, so I got a few of the best ones and Blu-tacked them into Grandad's scrapbook. I'd bought it from the village shop and it was really thick with coloured sugar-paper pages and a steam train on the front.

Next to where I'd stuck in the photos I wrote little reminders at the side of them in biro about who, where, when, what, that kind of thing.

We kept going back. Further and further back. Until eventually, when I turned a page of one of the albums, I found the photo of me and Grandad collecting fossils on the beach near our house. The first picture there was with me in it.

Grandad looked confused as he leafed back through the album. He must have realized some were missing. He raised an eyebrow at me. "Where are the others? From when we first met? The camp in Bosnia."

I could have told him that I hid them. Hid them in the box under my bed with all the other stuff. That they were from my other life. The one I didn't want to remember. . .

But I think he must have understood from the look on my face, because he gave a slight nod and then returned to the album.

So we kept going back. There was Leonard in red wellies sticking Grandad's pipe in a snowman. Victoria on a toy telephone wearing a fairy costume. Mum and Dad all dressed up and dancing. Grandad pulling a funny face while Leonard held up a pumpkin lantern with jagged teeth. Leonard, Victoria. Victoria, Leonard.

The further back we went, the weird thing was, the clearer things seemed to Grandad. The longer ago it was, the more he could tell me about it and the more detail he went into.

"I can remember that as if it were yesterday," he said.

We kept going back. Back further and further still. To before Dad and Mum met. Grandad got younger and younger. He had more and more hair with less and less grey in it. His wrinkles started to smooth out; he stood more upright, less hunched up. But you could tell it was him. He had the same cheeky grin, and I teased him that he was wearing the same cardigan he still wore now, only with no patches on the elbows.

*When was this?* I asked him. *What's going on?* And he could tell me, and I really felt I was getting somewhere. At first.

Two days went by. He seemed to be repeating himself less. He said nothing about his invisible stalker or Moggy the cat. Even Dad commented how Grandad seemed less grumpy. The swelling round his eye went down and the bruise got smaller.

And there was no mention whatsoever from Mum or Dad about Saturday afternoon or the Sunflower Care Home.

Leonard, of course, had to try and spoil things.

"If you think that'll save his last few brain cells, you're more stupid than you look, Bosnia Boy."

But, like I said, I really felt I was getting somewhere.

That is, until Mum gave me that album.

It was Tuesday morning. Grandad and I were sitting at the kitchen table, rain streaming down the patio doors, making jokes about his teenage hairstyle, when Mum came in carrying a thick book. The album was one I'd never seen before. She said she'd hunted it out from somewhere, and from the dust on the cover, I guessed it hadn't been looked at for years. It was the old-fashioned kind that had little sticky squares holding the photos by the corners, and sheets of tissue paper between its black pages. We took the album to the Den so we could look at it in peace, away from Leonard's scowling and Sophie's felt tips. Wrapped it in a plastic bag and made a dash for it.

We put the album on the tea chest and sat around it on our rickety chairs. On a special gold-edged page at the front of the album was a photograph of a woman, smiling at the camera, and written beside it in white pencil was "*Freda. Aged 19*". She was pretty. Her eyes looked sparkly and kind.

Grandad was very still, running a finger gently round the picture. He let out a long sigh, and said, more to himself than to me, "The last portrait I ever took. . ."

His voice trailed off.

"What was she like, Grandad?" I asked. "My grandma?"

Grandad sat back. It was a bit before he answered, but his eyes were bright, sort of happy and sad at the same time, and his voice went all strange.

"An angel, she was, Alex. That's what our Freda was. I still miss her. There's not a day goes by when I don't think about her."

I saw his face screw up like he'd hurt himself, and then he turned away from me.

After all these years he still missed my grandma. It was hard for him to even talk about her. Probably he'd never stop missing her, never stop feeling pain, unless. . . Unless he forgot who she was. He'd forgotten who I was, that day on the cliff. Would he forget her too one day? Would it be easier for him if he did forget her?

I knew one thing. It was easier for me to forget my past.

Much easier.

We leafed through some more pages.

There were photos of Grandad and Grandma's wedding. They were dated *1941*. I studied the curly writing. Yes, definitely. That was strange.

"You married Grandma in nineteen forty-one?" I asked.

"Nineteen forty-one. I remember it clear as a bell. January, it was. The church was freezing. It was mad to have a wedding in the middle of winter!"

I thought back. The photo in Dad's study of Grandma and Grandad's wedding had said *1940*, hadn't it? It must have had the wrong date on it.

We carried on looking at the album.

Grandad could tell me what the little pictures on the place settings at his wedding were (bluebirds), who had worn the most hideous hat (Great-Aunt Mildred with her wax fruit and roses), and how many glasses of home-made dandelion champagne he'd had to drink (ruddy war rationing, although he wasn't one hundred per cent sure he could trust his memory on that one!).

There was Grandma sitting at a writing desk, pen in hand. There was Grandma lifting Dad out of his cradle. There were photos of Grandma holding Dad as a baby, Great-Aunt Mildred holding Dad as a baby, and loads of Dad as a baby in general, doing the usual baby things. Grandad made a joke that Dad, even at that age, was dressed like he was ready to spend all day in the office, but he was generally more quiet, made fewer comments, even looked at some pages without saying a single thing. Some moments, the only sound was the rain drumming loudly on the windows. I guessed he was thinking about Grandma again.

A face we came across looked like a really young version of Miss Kirby.

"Yes, that's Hatty Kirby," Grandad told me. "Your grandma's best friend. That's Mildred in the background, with Henry Webb. They were engaged, those two, would you believe? Nice chap, that Henry. Nothing like his brother."

He turned the page. There was a photo of a man. I'd seen that face somewhere before. He looked like Grandad, but. . .

"That's our Tommie," said Grandad. He had the same expression as he did when he had been talking about Grandma. "My brother. Your great-uncle. Very close we were. Me and Tommie."

It clicked where I'd seen Tommie before! On that wedding photo in Dad's study, of course. The one with the wrong date. At first I'd thought it was Grandad standing there with Grandma in the picture, but now I realized it was Tommie.

So the photo in Dad's study was Grandma posing with her new brother-in-law. It was pretty odd, though, Dad having a photo of Grandma with Tommie, not Grandad. Maybe it was because Grandad was behind the camera doing his own wedding photos! Knowing Grandad, I wouldn't have been surprised.

I was about to ask him, but Grandad had already turned the page, and we suddenly came across a photo of Tommie in army uniform with a gun rested along his arm.

I felt images flick at the edge of my mind. Men with guns. . .

I flipped the page quickly. "Were you a soldier, Grandad?"

Grandad made a noise that could have been either yes or no, and then he closed the album. "I don't want to look at more now."

"But Grandad," I said, opening up the album again, "we haven't finished."

Grandad pressed the cover down with his fist. "I said I

don't feel like it! I don't like you asking all these questions!"

Rain pounded on the roof overhead. The images in my head were getting stronger. There were noises now too. Heavy boots on mud. Shouts. I felt my skin crawl as I tried to block them out.

Grandad had never tried to push me to say things I didn't want to, and here was me trying to make him tell me stuff. I was Stupid Tie Man with my black leather settee and certificates in gold frames on the wall. I wanted to leave him alone, but I knew I had to go on. I had to make the scrapbook. I had to keep my promise.

The trouble was, sitting there, going back through Grandad's life with him, it was making my past come back too. My past, waiting in the shadows like an enemy. Waiting to jump out on me. Ambush me.

I felt the old familiar panic grow inside me. I forced myself to think calmly. *This is for Grandad*, I told myself. *We've got less than four days.*

"Come on!" I said to him. "You've not told me anything about the war. Surely you can remember. . ."

He pulled the album away from me and spread a hand over the front.

"What's the point? I can't remember what I did yesterday, never mind what I did during the war!" He stood up, all agitated. "How do you expect me to remember what I did in the war? All I know is I didn't fight and I didn't have to shoot anyone!"

"OK, Grandad. Sit down."

"I told you, Alex. I'm not talking about that."

"I said OK."

Grandad sat down, breathing heavily, the bruise under his eye looking red and sore. Slowly, the bad stuff in my head faded. I felt guilty I'd got him so wound up. I made us an extra strong cup of tea and got out a packet of chocolate digestives.

Grandad must have felt guilty too, about the way he'd reacted, because after a bit he put down his tea, opened the album again and started turning the pages.

"Freda, Tommie, Hatty . . . Ruddy Mildred with her Henry. . ." He gave a short laugh. "Seems like only yesterday. Where's that tea you promised, Alex?"

I pushed his half empty mug towards him.

Grandad turned a page, and his face changed so much that I let the digestive I was dunking fall straight into my tea.

"What's *he* doing in there?"

I looked to see what had upset him so much. It was a shot of Tommie and Freda sitting on the riverbank grinning. There was a man I didn't recognize next to them. Grandad flipped the page, bending the corner in his hurry. On the next sheet was the same man, a cigarette between his teeth.

"I'm not having him in there! I'm not standing for it."

"Who is he?" I said.

"Never you mind, Alex."

The next thing I knew, Grandad was pulling at the photo. Before I had time to react, there was a tearing sound as the picture came away, taking most of the page with it.

"Grandad!"

"It's no place there," he said. He screwed up the photo and tossed it to the floor.

"I don't like you asking all these questions, I said, especially not about my Freda!" He got up. "Anyway, I can't sit around here idling. I've got much more important things to do!"

He strode towards the door, then stood there a moment like he was trying to remember what all those important things were. He went over to the gramophone as if he'd forgotten I was there and took a record from the pile. He slid the black disc from its sleeve and held it between two palms, studying its label. He put it on the turntable, set it going and lifted the needle on to it.

There was a scratching sound as the record spun, then familiar music. It was one Grandad played all the time. A woman started to sing. Vera Lynn.

*"There'll be bluebirds over, the white cliffs of Dover. . ."*

Grandad slumped down in the armchair and closed his eyes.

I watched him, but he didn't stir, so I quietly got a bit of sellotape and fixed the torn up photo as best I could. When Mum had said I could take photos out of the albums, this definitely wouldn't have been what she had in mind.

Why had Grandad reacted like that, anyway? Who was the man in the picture and what had he done to make Grandad so angry, even after all these years?

I checked Grandad still had his eyes shut and turned the photo over. There was some of that curly handwriting they used back then that I found really hard to read. The rips right through the words didn't help.

## *Pet Vel has a smk*

Somebody has a smoke? Let Vel? I couldn't make any sense of it. I looked at the photo again. The man was kind of hunched up with his cigarette, like there was something wrong with his shoulders. Something caught my eye. Something in the buttonhole of the man's jacket. It was a dark flower. Had to be red. A red carnation.

"They're after me."

I jumped, startled. Grandad was right by me, whispering. I hadn't heard him get up out of his chair. He edged over to where rain streamed down the windowpane and eased the curtain closed.

"Trying to get rid of the evidence, they are." He looked angry. Scared.

The woman's singing filled the room.

"*. . .And Jimmy will go to sleep*

*In his own little room. . .*"

Grandad's face relaxed again and he clapped his hands

and rubbed them together. "Where's that tea you promised me, eh, Alex?"

I looked at Grandad.

He looked back at me, grinning.

"You already drank it," I said.

# 8

# Mr Webb

*Bottom of the garden. Tuesday, 1:15 p.m. Trying to keep a clear head.*

L ia pulled up her hood and rotated herself round and round in her chair, studying the sellotaped photograph. Her wheels made muddy circles on our soggy end lawn.

The river was high because of all the rain. Water dripped off the branches of the willow trees, making tiny dints on the fast-moving surface. I kept my distance, eyeing the way the water churned at the tops of the banks. Our old rowing boat, the *Little Swift*, bobbed up and down, straining against its mooring rope. It looked about ready to sink.

I offered Lia the half empty packet of chocolate digestives I'd smuggled out of the Den. She handed back the mended photo I'd been showing her and took a biscuit.

"All this stuff about your grandad doesn't make any sense to me either," she said.

I licked the chocolate on the top of my biscuit. "The

weird thing is, Grandad seems to remember the stuff from years ago better than the stuff from last week."

"Yes!" Lia wagged a finger at me. "That's classic Alzheimer's. I read about that somewhere. Apparently that's what happens. People can think they're living back when they were loads younger. They truly believe it. I read a story about an eighty-year-old woman who got up one morning and went off to work in the local factory where she'd worked when she was nineteen. Course, the factory wasn't even there any more. It must have been a real shock when she found out."

Lia bit into her biscuit. "Well," she munched, "what I'm getting at is that maybe your grandad sometimes thinks he's back in the past somewhere and. . ." She finished her mouthful. "He's kind of reliving things that happened to him."

"Like Moggy," I said.

"Exactly. All that stuff about being watched, and people out to get him. It might not really be happening now, but maybe it did once in the past."

I nodded. It kind of made sense. "He said they were trying to get rid of the evidence."

"Yes, well, I also read somewhere that paranoia can be a symptom of Alzheimer's, you know, when you think people are after you but you're just imagining it? But what if maybe someone *was* after him, years ago, and that's what he meant."

I nodded again, but I wasn't so sure. I'd definitely seen

a figure in that photograph Grandad had developed, hadn't I? And that was from a few days ago, not a few decades.

The rain started to pour down again and the wind sent small branches tumbling from the willows.

"Come on, we'll get soaked!"

I ran, pushing Lia round to the front of the house and into the porch, and we stayed there, watching the rain against the glass.

There was a jumble of sounds from inside the house. Mum's orchestral CD. Victoria's Radio One I'll-take-as-long-as-I-like-in-the-bathroom clatter. The shooting and explosions of Leonard's computer games. Nothing from Dad — he was at work as usual. Sophie singing "I'm a princess! I'm a fairy princess!" at the top of her lungs.

"The big question is. . ." Lia used her elbow to rub condensation off the glass. "What has your grandad actually forgotten, and. . ." She stopped to look me right in the face. ". . .what does he remember but he's deliberately trying to forget?"

"Eh?" Lia did my head in sometimes.

"You know! Stuff he remembers, but doesn't want to talk about!"

I shrugged at her.

"It's like that locked room at the top of your house," Lia went on. "The one that Sophie thinks is full of crocodiles and tarantulas."

"But what has that got to do with anything?" I said,

trying not to think of Grandad's outburst after the ripped pillow incident. "It's got rotten floorboards, that's what Mum says, and the key was lost years ago."

Lia tapped her head. "Well, you see, which of Grandad's rooms up here have *really* lost their keys, and which keys is Grandad *pretending* he's lost?"

What was Lia going on about now? Locked rooms in your head? Keys? I was the one who was lost.

Lia waggled the sellotaped photo at me. "Tommie and Freda and this bloke, they're the key to all this, I reckon. If your grandad won't tell you about them, you'll have to find out for yourself." She drew a frowning face in the condensation. "Start with what you do know. Tommie?"

"Killed in France during the war," I said.

"Well, he'll be buried abroad, so we can't look for his gravestone so easily. That leaves your grandma. When did she die? Where's she buried? Must be in our graveyard, right?"

I shrugged. All I knew was that Grandma had died when Dad was really little.

"Can't you just ask your mum or dad?" said Lia.

"I'm not asking them anything!" I said. I felt a fresh wave of anger at their scheming over Grandad. "I'll find out myself! Besides, Dad always clams up when there's any mention of Grandma."

"Ask your grandad then."

I shook my head. "He got massively upset the last time I asked too many questions. He said he didn't want to talk about Grandma. Do you want me to wind him up even more?"

"OK, OK," Lia soothed. She blew the fringe from her eyes. "Wow, do your family never discuss anything?"

"How would finding Grandma's grave help anyway?" I said grumpily.

She handed me back the photo. "I don't know, but you have to start somewhere!"

I had an uneasy feeling. Was it right to dig up all the memories? I thought. Weren't there some it was best to keep hidden?

Look at how Grandad had reacted when I'd tried to force him into telling me things. And all that war stuff, it had got to me too.

Maybe it was better to forget. Keep the memories buried.

"I'm just not too sure it's a good idea," I mumbled.

Lia came close to me. "Don't you get it, Alex?" Her cheeks were flushed and she sounded angry. "You have to find out, for the scrapbook. A life isn't only happy stuff, is it? It's not only the stuff you get in holiday snaps. It's the bad things too. The stuff you want to shove in a box and never look at again!"

She was giving me this really hard stare when she said the thing about the box.

*Shut it, Lia*, I thought. *Leave me out of this*. I wished I'd never told her about the box under my bed. *Just shut it*.

I turned away from her and watched the river churn by. A tree trunk floated past and my mind made it into a body, face down in the water. *Not now*, I told myself. *Focus on Grandad*.

Lia sighed. "Look, Alex, all I'm saying is this scrapbook thing, well, if there's not very nice stuff in your grandad's memories, that's still part of who he is, surely? If you could find out why he's so upset and get him to talk about it, then he might open up about other things."

"Maybe," I said, still not looking at her. I knew she was right, but I didn't want to admit it.

"Look." Lia jabbed a finger into my arm and it hurt. "Do you want to make this scrapbook or not?"

I pulled myself out of my brooding. We only had until Saturday. What was I doing? I gave her a punch back and made an effort to think.

"In the church, there's a big list of names and dates," I said. "You know the one? All the people from the village who died in the war. Tommie should be on it." I put the sellotaped photo into my pocket. "I'll look around the graveyard first to see if Grandma's buried there, and then I'll check the list out."

Lia spun her chair round. "Go for it!"

A car horn blared in the street. She stopped, mid-turn, and her face fell.

"There's my dad. Right on time! Him and his stupid antiques! Why I always have to go with him, I don't know." She went to the door. "Look, I'll phone you when I can. Tell me what you find out, OK?"

\*

I started from the edge of the church lawns and walked slowly between the wet headstones. *Freda Smith*, I muttered to myself as I read the inscriptions. *Freda Smith*.

The first rows of graves with their glossy marble and rectangles of freshly sprouting grass were obviously too new to be Grandma's. I found a Karen Smith and a Rachel Smith, etched in glinting gold letters. I walked deeper in. The path snaked from one gravestone to another between big beech trees with thick, grooved trunks. Overhead, branches wobbled in the wind, caging me in. I read inscription after inscription. No Freda.

The damp grass became knee-high in places. My jeans clung to me as I forced my way through. Nettles stung at my ankles and I stumbled where tree roots made the ground all lumpy. More gravestones, more inscriptions, but the marble was pitted now and dark lichens grew in clots around the faded letters and numbers. Still nothing.

I smacked down, bashing my hands. I'd tripped over a tiny headstone, sunk into the ground as if it were slowly disappearing into quicksand. A baby? I stepped over it with a shudder and hurried on.

I thought about the boy's grave I'd seen on the day of the church fête, the vandalized headstone with the broken angel. I would have struggled to find that bit of the graveyard again. The path forked, and then forked again into nothing more than a mud track. I doubled back, tried another trail. More graves appeared from the shadows, none of them Grandma's. I lost my bearings and started to go round in circles.

I bent over to wriggle through a rhododendron bush. On the other side a piece of bramble lashed at my face. This was impossible! I was going to have to ask Grandad where Grandma's grave was after all, I told myself angrily. Whether he liked it or not. Tough! I headed in what I hoped was the right direction, and finally managed to find the main path back.

Mr Webb was limping about the church lawns with a pair of gardening shears and talking to himself. His anorak billowed about as he hacked at the damp hedges and the wind sent the bits flying.

I sneezed. I pulled out a tissue from my pocket and the sellotaped photo fell out with it. As I reached down for the picture, a breeze sent it flapping over the grass. I went to grab it, but it scuttled away from me again and before I could stop it, it had ended up right at Mr Webb's feet.

I stopped dead.

Slowly Mr Webb bent down and picked the photo up. He stared at it, then at me, then at the photo again, and his face went a sort of reddish purple colour. He started having some sort of coughing fit and staggering about. I went forward and reached out a hand to steady him, but he shook me off angrily.

"You're the Smith boy." It was as if he were accusing me of something. "The adopted one."

I didn't think it was any of his business.

"Could I have that back, please?"

He kicked over a stone with one foot and woodlice scuttled under it. He held up the photo. "What're you doing with this?"

I was over trying to be nice. "Give it back, will you?"

He stepped away from me, holding the photo out of reach.

"You're William Smith's grandson," he said, and from the way he said the name it was obvious Grandad wasn't his favourite person.

"I'm trying to find a few things out," I said. I had to say something. I wanted to get the photo back and get away from him. "Family histories and all that. It's a project for school."

Mr Webb stared hard at me. "It is, is it? Trying to find things out about William Smith's history, are you?" He drove the point of his shears into the wet grass.

"How about this, then?" His lips curled into a sneer. "A conchie he was. A ruddy, dirty conchie."

I stood there staring at him.

He coughed into his hand and wiped it on his trousers.

"Those photos he took! A slur on my brother's memory, they were. A slur on my Henry's memory!"

What was he going on about? What was a conchie? Which photos? Did he mean the ones at the fête? How could a lighthouse on a white cliff or a close-up of tree bark slur anyone's memory? What had they to do with Mr Webb's brother, Henry?

"Grandad develops photos all the time," I said. "There's nothing wrong with that!"

Mr Webb looked shocked. "So he's got more of them, eh?" He came closer. "He's up to his old tricks, then!" His face was right up to me now and I could see the gaps in his teeth. There was a curled up red flower in his breast pocket. He pressed his fingers against his forehead. I could see the dirt under his nails.

"Betrayed his brother during the war, know about that, do you?" He was spitting as he said the words. "Went and got his brother Tommie killed, he did."

I could hardly take in what I was hearing. It was hard to believe that seeing one photo had brought all this on.

"That makes him a *murderer*, that does," Mr Webb ranted.

The wind caught his anorak, making one shoulder billow upwards.

Memories hit me. The weirdly sloping shoulders of the figure in the photo hanging in Grandad's darkroom. . .

*I've got proof you're hounding me!*

. . .Grandad's black eye. Mr Webb's bandaged fist. . .

. . .Grandad in the tangle of weeping willow branches. A word caught in the air. . . *Murder*.

Everything suddenly seemed to fit.

"Are you following my grandad?" I blurted.

Mr Webb took a step away from me and narrowed his eyes. "Keep your nose out!" he hissed. "It doesn't concern you, boy."

So it *was* him.

"It doesn't concern you. Do you hear?"

I launched myself forward and made a swipe for the photo. Somehow I got it out of his claw-like hand and I made a run for it. When I glanced back he had picked up the gardening shears and was waving them about. I legged it across the lawns and round the side of the church. I saw the main door and wrestled with its big metal handle. It wouldn't turn. I tugged and twisted and finally it gave and the door swung open with a horrible creak. I rushed in, pulling it shut behind me.

Immediately I regretted what I'd done. The church was empty. I was trapped in there. I ran up the dark aisle looking for a place to hide. Behind me was the clattering sound of the handle turning, the door squealing open. I dived between the benches and rolled myself under one, chest heaving against the cold stone floor. I made myself as small as I could and squeezed my eyes tight shut.

I heard the door swing wider, then close with a heavy thump.

Footsteps.

Getting closer.

I put my fists to my face, desperately trying to block the images that were seeping into my head. But I couldn't stop them. . .

. . .*I hear the thumping of heavy boots. Feel the mud splash my face as the men run past where we're hiding. Nicu and me. Curled up in the cold mud, the smallest we can be.* . .

I don't know how long I was under the church bench for. I opened my eyes. I saw jagged patches of red light from stained-glass windows lighting the floor. The church was completely silent. I stayed there a while longer and then slowly uncurled my numb body and edged forward on my stomach, peering out.

The dead people caught my eye. The lists of names I'd told Lia about. The men from our village killed in the war. Light from candles on a tall stand flickered over the wood panels, making the gold letters stand out.

I scoured up the lists. . . *1945. . . 1944. . . 1943. . . 1942 . . . 1941. . .*

1940.

There were more people listed under that date than any of the others. There were plenty of Smiths there. . . Stanley, Robert, David, Samuel. . . I couldn't see anybody called Thomas. I kept reading. I caught my breath. *Webb. Henry Webb.*

Before I could think more about it, there was a voice, a whisper. Very, very near to me.

"Come on out now. I know you're there."

# 9

# Reverend Posselthwaite

*In church. 4:40 p.m. Divine inspiration.*

Reverend Posselthwaite got up from where he'd been kneeling. He clasped his hands together and looked at me through his thick glasses as I dusted myself off.

"How's the family, Alex?" he asked cheerfully, as if nothing had happened and he hadn't just found me poking my head out from under one of his church benches.

"Fine," I said, forcing a smile.

"I popped in to have a word with. . ." The vicar pointed at the ceiling. ". . .you-know-who."

I stood there and nodded. My mind was still spinning from all the things Mr Webb had said.

"If the weather clears up I'll take my rubbing." Reverend Posselthwaite straightened his glasses and pulled up a big sheet of what looked like thick tracing paper and a tin of posh wax crayons. "We recently lost a parishioner, much to our sorrow. Here one minute, gone the next. So there's a new headstone to add to the records."

He must have seen the look of confusion on my face. "I make a copy of all the new headstones in the graveyard," he announced, looking pleased with himself. "I carry on the parish tradition, albeit a sad one. As you know, I haven't been here very long. Anyway, a predecessor of mine, a Reverend Bartholomew Bath – a fine name, if ever I heard one – he started the idea off, and all the vicars who have come to the parish ever since have continued his work."

A thought came to me. Why not ask Reverend Posselthwaite if he knew where Grandma was buried?

"Don't *you* know?" He scratched his head at my question. "Can't say I do. And so much of the graveyard's older sections are overgrown at the moment. The rhododendrons and brambles take over so fast. It's an enormous area to look after. An ongoing battle! I've been asking for volunteers to tame the jungle. Mildred offered your family's services, in fact." He gave me a wink. "No doubt she'll be letting you know about that in due course.

"But rest assured, Alex, every rubbing has the exact position of the grave written in the top left corner. So all we must do is find the rubbing from your grandma's grave and we'll automatically know where the grave is! What was her name again?"

"Freda Smith."

He nodded happily. "The rubbings are all ordered alphabetically."

"I've time now," I said. "If you're not too busy?"

"Come along then!" he said excitedly. "I keep the collection in my study. My wife has made some excellent fruit scones and I dare say she could find us something to drink and a spot of home-made jam!"

We walked out of the church and across the wet grass towards his house. I kept looking over my shoulder, but there was no sign of Mr Webb anywhere.

All I could think about was what he'd said about Grandad.

I swallowed. I tried to sound casual. "What's a conchie?" I asked.

Reverend Posselthwaite stopped and looked at me.

"It's for a school project," I said, staring at my feet.

He cleared his throat. "Ah, well, *conchie* is a slang word for a *conscientious objector*. That's somebody who refuses to fight in a war, for moral reasons.

"In the Second World War, for example, a person could say they were a conscientious objector, and instead of being a soldier they would have to work in a factory or farm or a hospital, wherever they were sent. Everyone was expected to help out with the war effort. If you said no, you'd be put in prison."

So if what Mr Webb had said was true, I thought, Grandad hadn't been a soldier during the war. I remembered his outburst in the Den. *I didn't fight, I didn't shoot anyone!*

We passed the memorial, a statue of soldiers surging from a boat, guns raised. *Our Finest Hour* was chiselled into a stone scroll at the bottom. One man had his head flung back and had dropped his gun and had a hand to his chest. Another was face down in water. There didn't seem to be anything fine about that.

"Dunkirk. Nineteen forty." Reverend Posselthwaite paused beside me. "A third of a million soldiers rescued from the beaches of northern France. Used as powerful propaganda to raise morale; I'm sure you know the story. But the evacuation was actually a huge defeat for the Allies and there were a good many people who never made it home."

He nodded sadly at the statue. "More boats went out to Dunkirk from here than anywhere else along this stretch of coast, don't you know? That's why this spot was chosen for such a big memorial."

There were wreaths of poppies propped up around the base, raindrops on their red paper petals.

"Very controversial it was," went on Reverend Posselthwaite, looking up at the stone figures. "Putting death into stone like that. I understand there were quite a number of locals who were very upset by the idea."

We got to the vicarage and I took off my shoes in the porch, but Reverend Posselthwaite was too busy thinking about getting to his study and left a trail of muddy footprints down the hall, which got him a good telling off from Mrs Posselthwaite, who appeared from the kitchen.

"Nice to see you, Alex," she greeted me with a smile. She looked down at my feet. "Now there's a well-educated young man!"

She rolled her eyes at her husband, and then bustled off.

The room Reverend Posselthwaite took me to was more like a library than a study. Tall bookcases lined all the walls, with the top shelves close to the ceiling and well out of reach. There was a huge desk in the middle of the room, covered in a thick jumble of papers and books, and one very large, very annoyed-looking, white Persian cat.

"The rubbings are all up there," he said, after he'd finished explaining his complex system of organization according to surname and then Christian name. He pointed vaguely at the top shelves. I could see masses of cardboard tubes and rolls of paper jutting out from them. "Freda Smith, wasn't it? Should be easy to find!"

Just then Mrs Posselthwaite came in carrying a tray with cups and plates and a steaming teapot. The vicar used his arm to sweep a space on the desk and the cat shifted position grumpily.

"There used to be a graveyard plan," he said. "But Tiddles here took a shine to it one day. Clawed it to shreds. I keep promising I'll do some tidying round here, don't I, dear?"

"I'll believe it when I see it, dear." Mrs Posselthwaite poured me some tea. "There you go, Alex." She pushed the milk jug and sugar bowl towards me. "How's the family? Your grandad?"

"Fine, thanks," I said.

"Remember that shirt's clean on, Harold." I imagined her ironing his shirts to cardboard perfection. "Strawberry all right, Alex?" She spooned a heap of jam on to one side of a buttered scone and added a blob of cream. "It's actually a jar your mum made. Delicious, it is."

Mrs Posselthwaite left.

"Now," said the vicar, adjusting his glasses. "Ah, yes, Freda Smith! But first things first." He took a swig from his cup and ended up dribbling tea all down the front of his shirt. "Oh dear me!" he cried cheerfully. "Mrs P. *will* be cross!"

He took a big bite out of his scone, adding jam stains to the tea and spilling crumbs all over the floor. The clock on the wall chimed. I wished he'd hurry up. There were so many things to find out about Grandad. Big chunks of his life were still a total mystery.

The vicar wiped his mouth on his sleeve. "Now, where were we?"

"My grandma's grave?"

"Do not fear! The complete rubbing will still be intact." He swept a hand towards the tubes on the shelves. "That's the beauty of the Reverend Bath system!"

He took a metal stepladder from behind the door and

opened it out. The ladder wobbled as he climbed up. A couple of cardboard tubes thudded down, narrowly missing my head.

"So sorry," called the vicar. "Now, let me see. Freda Smith, you say?" He peered at the handwritten names on the outsides of the tubes. "Jeffreys . . . Jenkins . . . Butterworth. . . Oh dear, the organization isn't quite what it should be."

He started pulling out tubes at random. "Wilkinson. . . Willows. . . This one hasn't got a name." He opened a tube and unrolled the paper from inside. "No, that's a drowning from 1835. Where are you, Freda Smith? I know you're up here somewhere!"

More tubes tumbled. The cat dived for cover.

Reverend Posselthwaite spent the best part of twenty minutes searching and still couldn't find the right piece of paper, but I couldn't hang around there any longer. I had to get home. Get things moving. Grandad could be angry if he wanted to, but I had to try and ask him about what Mr Webb had said.

"The rubbing will definitely be on the shelves somewhere, Alex," Reverend Posselthwaite said to me at the door as I pulled my shoes back on. "It might just take me a little bit of time to locate. Soon as I find it, I'll let you know!"

He waved at me through the window as I went down the drive.

I broke into a jog.

Conchie. Grandad's photos. Getting his brother, Tommie, killed.

Grandad wouldn't hurt a fly. But there was Mr Webb accusing him of all sorts of terrible things.

My brain felt in such a mess. More of a mess than Reverend Posselthwaite's study.

But the chaos of the vicar's study was nothing compared to what I found when I got home.

# 10

# Messed Up

*At home. 5:20 p.m. Chaos revisited.*

G randad met me at the door. He looked in a right
state.

"They followed me to the Den," he told me,
wide-eyed, his painful-looking purple lid all stretched.
"Didn't find it, though. Thank God they didn't find it." He
gripped me. "I promised Tommie, see. I promised
Tommie!"

"Come on now. That's enough." Dad shepherded
Grandad into the kitchen and sat him down.

"There's been burgers!" shouted Sophie, jumping up
and down. "Burgers!"

Mum scooted around pouring gigantic glasses of orange
juice for everyone, as if everything would be all right if we
all just had a good strong dose of vitamin C.

Dad was still in his work jacket and looked really
hassled. "Can we all sit down and calm down!"

Leonard pinched my arm under the table. "Enjoyed

vandalizing Grandad's darkroom, did you, Bosnia Boy?" he said in a hard whisper.

I shoved him. "I don't know what you're on about."

"Yeah, right," said Leonard.

"Thank God they didn't find it," Grandad said to me from across the table. I stroked his hand.

"Grandad's darkroom got messed up?" I said.

"As if you didn't know," muttered Leonard.

"Your grandad says that somebody broke in trying to steal something," said Dad. "He won't tell us what. A couple of bottles of chemicals got smashed. The room's in a terrible state."

"We'll have to call the police," said Mum.

"I've no intention of calling the police," said Dad.

"Why not?"

Dad drew her aside and lowered his voice, but he was so wound up I could hear every word.

"Because he obviously did it himself, Hilary."

Mum frowned at him. "Now why would William. . ."

"He's getting more unbalanced as the days go on," Dad went on. "There's no sign of a forced entry, and only he has the key to the padlock on the door, so who else could it have been?"

I felt my blood boil. How could Dad think Grandad would do something like that? Why would he? But then I remembered the vicious way Grandad had yanked the photograph from the album and ripped it up.

I thought about Mr Webb. The anger in his voice

when he'd talked about Grandad's photos. His reaction when he thought Grandad had been developing more of them.

It had to have been Mr Webb. It had to have been. I wanted to believe it was him, not Grandad. But I knew Mr Webb would have had to act fast if he'd left me, magically broken into Grandad's darkroom and turned the place over, all before I got back from the vicar's house. With that bad limp of his, I doubted he could have broken into a run, never mind anything else.

Leonard slouched out.

"People in the village have been talking." Grandad leaned towards me. "But let them think what they want, that's what I say. They don't want to hear the truth anyway. Ruddy gossips, they are, the lot of them."

"He's a danger to himself here, Hilary," I heard Dad say. "We have to do what's best for him."

Mum filled a pan with water and clattered it on to the hob. She lit the gas and blue flames sprang up at its base.

Grandad gazed at the flames, then looked at me all agitated. "It was on fire. It was all on fire." He was trembling, getting hysterical. "I was on my way home. Saw the smoke. . ."

I held on to his hand more tightly. "It's OK," I said. "Shhhh."

"My Freda and the baby were in there!"

"It's OK, Grandad." He wasn't making any sense. What was this about a fire?

109

"Alex, I need to talk to you." Dad's voice cut across the kitchen, and he was telling, not asking. He strode to the door.

"But. . ."

"Now."

I squeezed Grandad's hand and then followed Dad into the hall.

He closed the kitchen door behind us.

We stood facing each other in the narrow space. I listened to the loud ticking of the grandfather clock.

"Look, Alex." Dad ran his fingers through his hair, what was left of it. "All this looking at old photos with your grandad, all this stirring up memories. . ."

"Mum said I could take photos out of the albums!" I protested. "I need them for Grandad's scrapbook."

"I know all that. I know about the scrapbook." Dad sighed. "It was a great idea, Alex, but. . ."

I didn't like the way he said "*was* a great idea", and I liked the "*but*" even less. I swallowed and waited for what he was going to come out with next.

"I want you to stop, Alex."

I gaped at him.

"I want you to stop with the photos and stop with the scrapbook," said Dad. "You thought you were doing the right thing, but it's not good for your grandad. All this being reminded about what happened to him in his life. He's been getting upset, confused. Look at what he did to his darkroom."

"But Dad!" I managed to splutter.

"You'll only upset him more," Dad said. He pretended to look like *he* was the one getting upset. Dad could be so false.

"Some things are best forgotten, Alex."

"I have to carry on!" I couldn't tell him about my promise. He wouldn't understand anyway. "Grandad likes his scrapbook!" I blurted. It sounded so lame.

"Listen to me, Alex."

"I have to carry on!"

"No."

I saw Leonard smiling down at me over the top banister. I wanted to slap his stupid face.

"It's helping Grandad," I shouted.

"I said no. You have to stop."

"You can't make me!"

"I forbid it, Alex, and that's the end of it!"

Leonard mimed hysterical laughter.

"If I find out you've been carrying on. . ."

I stood there, not trusting myself to speak.

Dad let out a sigh. "But if ever you want to talk, Alex . . . about anything. . ." His voice trailed off. "Well, you know where I am." He strode away into his study and shut the door.

Leonard stuck out his bottom lip and waved at me over the banister. I heard his feet on the landing and his bedroom door bang.

I stayed there trembling. The ticking of the grandfather

clock down the hall seemed to get louder and louder until it was drilling right into my skull.

I pressed my hands over my ears. I'd promised Grandad, and finally I was starting to find out the truth. If I stopped now, it would all be for nothing.

When were Dad and Mum going to tell the rest of us what they'd got planned for Grandad, anyway? I thought furiously. They hadn't even told Grandad that come Saturday he'd be saying goodbye to the only place that had ever been home for him. They didn't even have the guts for that.

Leonard's taunts came back to me. *"Get packing, Bosnia Boy."*

What was to stop them one day saying, out of the blue, *We're fed up with you now, Alex. We've decided to get rid of you next week.*

They weren't going to do anything to help Grandad. They were happy to sit back and let it happen, or pretend it wasn't happening at all. Now they were even stopping me from doing something to help.

I found the darkest end of the hall and crouched there, pressing my forehead against the wall.

I'd been stupid to start all this in the first place. What had I been thinking, anyway? Make a scrapbook of Grandad's life? Trap all his memories in it? Did I honestly think that would stop him being taken away?

It was like trying to make a cage for your memories. A memory cage to stop them getting away. But memories

112

don't want to be trapped. They slip between the bars. Like smoke, like water.

They get in, as well as out.

I knew that. Better than anyone.

But what were you if you didn't have memories? Memories were what made you who you were. If you lost your memories, you lost yourself.

You were nothing.

A ghost.

Without memories, you didn't exist.

I kicked at the wall. Thumped it with my fists. It hurt, but I didn't care. I hit the wall again. And again. There was blood on my knuckles, but I hardly noticed. I hated them all. They were going to put Grandad in a home. They were getting rid of him like some old bit of junk for a charity shop. But that *wasn't* the end of it. Not by a long way.

I leaned against the wall, panting.

I was going to keep making the scrapbook and they could just try and stop me! I'd made a promise to Grandad and I was going to do whatever it took to keep it.

And if Dad found out?

I had to make sure he didn't.

"I suggest you take your father's advice."

I whipped round to see who'd spoken, and there in the hallway, jabbing her walking stick towards me, false teeth clenched, was Great-Aunt Mildred.

# 11

# The Grandfather Clock

*In the hallway. 5:35 p.m. A ticking off.*

"Take your father's advice," Great-Aunt Mildred snapped. "Stop stirring up the past."

She pointed her stick at my fist mark on the paintwork. "And you can stop that destructive behaviour right now, boy." She spoke slowly and loudly, as if I were hard of hearing and didn't know English. "We don't do that sort of thing in civilized countries, you know.

"I let myself in, seeing as the front door was open," she said. "I've got better things to do than wait on your front step in the pouring rain knocking and being ignored, and with all the din going on and the clattering about in the kitchen, it's no wonder nobody heard me."

*Nosy Old Bat*, I thought. *What's wrong with waiting in the porch?* But then I realized our unfriendly fake Great-Aunt Mildred must know something about Grandad's time during the war. She had to. And there wasn't any time for polite chit-chat. I plunged in with my question.

"What happened to Grandad's brother, Tommie?"

Great-Aunt Mildred looked at me hard and made a clacking sound with her false teeth. "Ah, now, there's a story," she said. "There's a real drama."

Couldn't she give me a straight answer?

"That's what you want to know about, is it? After all these years. . ." Great-Aunt Mildred looked around to check nobody was about. "I promised your father I wouldn't say anything." She glanced towards the closed door of Dad's study.

"But you go raking up the past and you get what you deserve, young man." She licked her lips, like she was on the beach about to open a packet of ham sandwiches that she'd been really looking forward to.

"Just tell me about Tommie," I said. "Please."

She leaned on her stick and eyed me.

"At first your grandad William didn't go to war at all. He pretended to have *principles*." She turned her nose up at the word. "He wasted his time on photography instead.

"Then he lured Tommie over to Dunkirk and got him killed."

I flinched. Two different people saying that Grandad had got his brother killed. Did that make it true? I imagined Great-Aunt Mildred gossiping over her garden hedge to her neighbours, spreading lies. That's what they were, weren't they? Big fat lies from people with nothing better to do.

"William even got a medal for bravery," Great-Aunt Mildred scoffed. "Can you believe that? The soldier who recommended him must have been bribed! Either that or he had shell shock!"

She gave out a short, dry laugh.

"William got everything, he did, once Tommie was dead. The house and everything in it."

What was she saying? That Grandad deliberately planned to get his brother killed so he could inherit the house?

Great-Aunt Mildred scowled. "The house wasn't the only thing he got his hands on."

She waddled down the hall and tapped her stick on the door of the grandfather clock. "Did you know that was a wedding present from your grandad to your grandma? Did you know that?" I shook my head and she puckered her lips.

"Yes, a wedding present to your grandma," she said in a harsh whisper. "For her *first* wedding, that is."

Great-Aunt Mildred came very close to me, and I could see her painted-on eyebrows and smell the sickly scent of her face cream. It was like the gone-off milk Grandad left out for Moggy.

Great-Aunt Mildred's eyes were bright. Her false teeth shone unnaturally white in the dimly lit hallway. "Once Tommie was out of the way," she whispered, "then our hero William came home to marry his brother's wife!"

She leaned back with satisfaction, watching my face.

I thought about the photo in Dad's study. Grandma and Tommie. 1940.

I struggled to get the facts straight in my head:

1. Grandma married Tommie in 1940.

2. Tommie died that same year.

3. Grandad married Grandma in 1941 (he'd told me that himself).

I didn't know how I felt about that. It was a bit weird, I thought, but there was nothing that wrong with what Grandad had done, was there? I mean, so what? But even I had to admit, it did seem a bit too soon after Tommie's death.

"How did Grandma die?"

Great-Aunt Mildred sniffed. Maybe she realized she'd got carried away and told me too much already. "Don't delve into things that aren't your business," she said.

Which I thought was rich coming from her.

"You'll not get any more out of me, boy." She began to shuffle off. "The past is done and dusted. Your father rightly put a stop to your scrapbook nonsense, and you should take his advice and leave well alone."

I watched her disappear into the kitchen and shut the door behind her.

First Mr Webb, now my foul aunt. All saying horrible things about Grandad. I had to find out the truth. What happened to him during the war was a big part of his life story. Too big a gap to leave out.

Lia was right. I had to get Grandad to tell me about it. And if he wouldn't, I had to find out for myself.

But why did there have to be so many secrets? There were too many. They were like brambles, scratching and choking, taking over, making cages round me. I felt closed in, like being in a coffin.

The loud ticking of the grandfather clock drummed on my brain. It seemed to be mocking me. *Tick, tock... Time's up, Alex. They're taking Grandad away...*

The ticking got louder and louder in my head until I couldn't stand it any more.

I wrenched open the door of the clock and stared at the mess of weights and chains inside. I thumped at the pendulum, and it rocked a little, then went back to its horrible ticking. I was about to punch it again, harder this time, when something caught my eye. Something glinted right in the bottom of the clock's cabinet.

I checked around. No Leonard spying through the banister, Dad's study door still tight shut. I heard Mum and Aunt Mildred's muffled voices coming from the kitchen, Sophie's not-so-muffled shrieks. Grandad conspicuous by his silence.

I reached a hand in and felt around with my fingertips, trying to keep my head out of the clockwork. I pulled out my hand, and when I opened it, there was a key in my palm.

At first I thought it must be the one that was used to wind the clock. But I saw that that key was already stuck in a hole in the dial.

The key I'd found was bigger. It was made of a faded

silvery metal. As soon as my hand closed around it, somehow I knew which door the key would unlock.

I didn't know why it had been hidden there or who had hidden it, but I knew what it was for.

I took it straight up to my bedroom and hid it under my pillow.

It was the key to the room of Sophie's cocodriles and transhlers.

The key to the locked, forbidden room at the top of our house.

## 12

# Photographic Memory

*Under the dining room table. Wednesday, 2 p.m. Head in a tangle.*

"Talk about secrets in the family," said Lia. "Your Uncle Tommie dies, and some people say your grandad was to blame; then he goes and marries his brother's wife virtually straight after!"

Rain thumped on the window beside me as I sat under the dining room table with the phone pressed against my head.

It was the first chance I'd had to talk to Lia, thanks to Great-Aunt Mildred making us work in the graveyard, cutting back rhododendron bushes. She'd kept pestering Mum about it yesterday, saying she'd promised the vicar, and *how would it look if we didn't turn up?* until Mum agreed that we'd help. Grandad had told me he'd rather chop off his own head and disappeared to the Den.

Dad was at work, of course, so he got out of it, and the whole morning was used up with Mum fussing about our drenched waterproofs and the dangers of garden clippers,

Aunt Mildred nagging, Leonard and Victoria whinging about the lukewarm tea and rubbish sandwiches, Sophie splashing in the mud and getting filthy. Me, trying not to think about all the time I was losing, my head in more of a tangle than the plants I was hacking. I kept an eye out for Freda Smith inscriptions, but no luck. I just hoped the vicar wouldn't forget about finding that rubbing.

So finally I'd got to phone Lia and fill her in. The only thing I missed out was the key. Don't ask me why. Maybe I should have told her absolutely everything. There were less than three days left till Grandad had to go into the home and I needed all the help I could get. But for some reason I held back on the key. Probably it was because I knew she'd say, "Open the door then, Alex! What are you waiting for? Why haven't you tried it already?"

The truth was, I wasn't ready to try that door. I'd hardly slept all night thinking about it. I didn't want to go in that room. I had a bad feeling about it. A really bad feeling.

"So, your grandad and Tommie were at Dunkirk in nineteen forty?" Lia paused. "I know about that battle. Dad's always spouting history at me. There were all these soldiers, thousands and thousands of them, who'd got trapped on the beaches in France, and they had nowhere safe to go and they were being bombed all the time, and all these people went over the Channel in their boats to rescue them. Just ordinary people. All sorts of boats there were, like yachts and fishing boats. It was pretty amazing. Loads of soldiers were saved."

I remembered Reverend Posselthwaite telling me about the Dunkirk memorial. What had he said? Something about a third of a million people being rescued . . . *there were a good many people who never made it home*.

"Loads died too, though, right?" I whispered down the mouthpiece.

"Yeah. It was pretty horrible. But there would have been thousands more dead if the boats hadn't gone."

We were both quiet a bit, and then Lia said, "I still can't believe that Mr Webb and Great-Aunt Mildred think your grandad killed your Uncle Tommie. He's supposed to have done it on purpose so he could marry your grandma? Seems a bit far-fetched! I mean, it was the middle of a battle. People were getting killed left, right and centre."

My jaw went tight. The perfect place to murder someone then, I thought.

Maybe Lia had exactly the same thought right then because she suddenly said, "Oh," and neither of us said anything for quite a while.

"Then I suppose your grandma and grandad had your dad," said Lia at last. "But your grandma died when he was still a baby, and all that's a mystery too. . . Hey, have you thought, maybe that's why your dad doesn't seem to like your grandad much? I mean, if your Great-Aunt Mildred helped bring your dad up, she could have said all sorts of horrible things to turn him against your grandad, like *'Did you know that your father got your Uncle Tommie killed?'* blah, blah. I mean, you didn't believe her, did you, because that stuff about your grandad, well, it can't be true, can it?"

I didn't answer. I didn't say, *Course not!* or *Don't be stupid!* I didn't know what to believe any more.

Lia whistled down the phone at me. "So you had to leg it from Mr Webb and his garden shears?" She giggled. "Maybe you were next in line for a good pruning!"

"It wasn't funny."

"Hey, Mr Webb said your grandad was a conchie?"

"Yes." I repeated the vicar's words. "A conscientious objector."

"Yes, Dad told me about those too. You wouldn't be the most popular person around, though, if you were one of those."

"What d'you mean?"

"Well, think about it! If your dad or brother or whoever were soldiers in a war, you might not like your local William Smith very much if he seems to be getting away with not fighting. Some people thought they were cowards."

"It wasn't like that, though, was it?" I said. "Conchies still did important jobs, right?"

"Yes. A lot of them worked in very dangerous situations, actually, alongside the soldiers, as medics or whatever. But I guess there were plenty of people who still didn't like the idea."

*Yes, Mr Webb for one*, I thought.

Lia sneezed and I heard her blow her nose. "Sounds like

your dad's pretty serious about you not carrying on with your grandad's scrapbook," she snuffled.

"I don't care," I told her. "I'm still going to finish it! But listen, we've got to be totally careful from now on. If Dad finds out. . ."

"Don't worry," said Lia. "My lips are sealed. I just wish I were there to help you more instead of having to work with Dad so much. Can you believe we've another antiques fair coming up? Military memorabilia, of all things."

She rang off. I wished she *was* there to help me.

I went to find Grandad. I had to get him to talk. To talk about what happened to him during the war. About being a conchie. About Tommie and Dunkirk. I had to try and fill the gaps. He wouldn't like it, but we didn't have any choice.

Grandad was in the Messing About Room. It was already gloomy in there. Outside it was all overcast and it was still raining, and the smoke from his pipe didn't exactly help.

He smiled as I went in. "Come and look at these, Alex."

I went over and turned on the lamp. Smoke spiralled up towards the bulb, looping and growing above his head into a grey, hovering haze.

Grandad had his tins of tea cards in front of him. He rooted around in one and picked out a pile. He took the elastic band from around it and fanned the cards on the table. *Flags of the World*. He did the same with *Cars* and *Kings of England*.

"All complete sets!" he said proudly. "Worth a few bob now, I shouldn't wonder!"

I didn't have the heart to jump straight in with my grilling. It probably wouldn't work anyway. How was I going to stop him either getting angry or clamming up? How was I going to get him to talk?

I had an idea.

I got him to put on a record and hunt out some biscuits, and while he was fiddling around with the mugs and tea bags, I scooped the cards off the table and replaced the pile with a different set I'd sneaked from another tin.

It was sly, I know, but I was desperate.

We settled back at the table with tea, and Vera Lynn on the gramophone, and I took the first tea card off the pile and laid it down.

The Battle of Little Bighorn, the Battle of Hastings, the Battle of Dunkirk. . .

Unfortunately he saw straight through my cunning plan.

"Forget it, Alex," he said stubbornly, gathering up the *Famous Battles of the World* cards.

"But you got a medal, Grandad," I persisted. "For bravery."

"Who told you that?" he snapped. "So what if I did?" He thumped the cards back into the tin. "I don't believe in medals. What are they? Bits of metal stuck on the chest of a corpse! There were plenty of boys far braver than I was who got nothing for what they did."

So much for my Plan A, I thought. I'd have to switch to Plan B.

I got out the album and casually turned to a photo of Tommie.

Grandad lifted the page up to his face and grinned a little.

"I told him not to let the barber cut his hair so short, but he never listens to me."

He looked at his watch. "He should be here any minute. We're going to the Officer for a pint."

I swallowed. Why was he talking about his brother as if he were still alive? I found myself looking nervously at the door.

I turned the pages, searching for another Tommie picture. There he was with my grandma having a picnic. I decided my burning question, *Grandad, did you kill your brother?* was a bit too blunt, and I was about to start with a more gentle way in, when I stopped. I peered at the print.

Tommie and Grandma were sitting on our back lawn, I realized. That was definitely our house in the background. But the reason I hadn't worked it out before was that there was another small building by the house, about where Mum's veggie patch was now. There was a huge tree too, between the smaller building and the house, an oak or something that was so tall it looked like its branches were touching our roof.

I must have had my finger on the building while I was staring at the photo because Grandad said, "That's my darkroom."

I looked at him. "But it's not there any more, Grandad," I said. "You've a darkroom further down the garden now, in your Den. That's where we are now!"

He looked blankly at me. He stared around the room. "Don't be daft!" He tapped the building on the photo. "That's my darkroom. What's this about a den?"

The stuff Grandad was coming out with was making me very nervous. I took hold of his hands. I decided it was now or never.

"Grandad. What happened at Dunkirk?"

"Eh?" He flinched, like I was scalding him.

I kept going, trying to keep my voice firm. "What happened to Tommie?"

He looked at me, long and hard. I saw a familiar stubborn look creep over his face.

"I don't remember."

"Try," I demanded. "Come on!"

I knew my voice was angry, and I could see he was getting upset, but Lia had said you had to remember the bad things too, hadn't she? The bad as well as the good.

I wanted to shake him. He must remember! Course he remembered. He just didn't want to.

"Leave me be, can't you?" said Grandad. "You're always getting at me! I can't remember any of that, all right?"

I looked at his face. Maybe it was true. Maybe he wasn't deliberately being difficult. Maybe he really was starting to forget the things from years ago that were once as clear as a bell. Maybe the Alzheimer's had taken a stronger grip over his mind than I thought.

I felt suddenly afraid and miserable. I was like that Canute, holding his hands up to try and stop the tide coming in. But it was impossible to stop the sea. Impossible to stop it smoothing the sand and wiping the beach flat. Stupid even to try.

What I was trying to do was impossible. I was as crazy as Canute.

Letters drawn out in sand came into my head.

*William Smith was here.* Moving water chiselling away the letters.

*Alex Smith was here.* The words crumbling into nothing.

"It's what's in here. . ." Grandad tapped his head angrily. "Don't you understand? It's what's in here that counts, and I'm losing it. I may as well be dead and buried, like my Tommie." His voice broke into a sob. "Dead and buried, like my Freda!"

He jumped up and started throwing things down. His mug of tea crashed down and broke; the biscuit plate smashed. He kicked at his pile of records and sent them scattering across the train tracks. Before I could stop him, our box of fossils had thudded down and there were pieces of broken rock all over the floor.

I rolled myself into a ball. The smallest curled-up shape I could. A pebble. A bullet. Hard and cold. Totally still. Trying not to even breathe. . .

. . .*But they have seen us. We run through the woods. I am gripping Nicu's hand, pulling him, the men with guns getting closer. . .*

*If only I hadn't stumbled. Made us slip down the bank into the river.*

*We are scrambling, tumbling, hitting the water. Its coldness suffocates me. I feel its strong press against my throat. Tree branches scratch at the top of my head. We are being dragged along. I remember water in my mouth, kicking wildly against the current. The river claws me under. . .*

*I remember the look in Nicu's eyes*

*I can never forget those eyes*

*the moment*

*I*

*let go*

*of*

*his*

*hand*

I squeezed my eyes shut. I couldn't stand it. I had to stop my memories coming back. I had to focus on Grandad's life. Finish his scrapbook. Keep my promise.

I had to sift through the fragments of his life. Piece them back together until the truth was lying there for everyone to see.

The past.

The truth.

Like a long-dead fossil in a chunk of cold, dead rock.

# 13

# Cocodriles and Transhlers

*My bedroom. Past midnight. All in the mind.*

I had a dream that night. Different from the others.

I was running through our house, frantically searching for something. I didn't know what, but I knew it had to be there somewhere. I had to find it. I just had to. It was a matter of life or death.

All the doors were closed and I was scrambling with the handles to get through them as fast as I could. But the more doors I opened, the more shut doors there seemed to be, and the rooms were filling with water. The water was gushing in through the walls, through the floor, the ceiling, and I was getting more and more desperate. There was water up to my knees as I scrambled about, and then it was up to my waist. Furniture floated around the room. Chairs and coffee tables and chests of drawers. I was trying to swim but my head kept going under.

I tried the last door handle, but it was locked. I tugged at it, screaming for help. I saw Grandad, sitting calmly on a floating armchair. The round table from the Den was floating next to him, with the gramophone on it playing a Vera Lynn record.

"Hello, Alex," he said. "Promise me you'll not let them take me away."

His hand stretched towards me, but instead of helping me out of the water, he was pushing me under.

"*Promise me.*"

I felt water go into my mouth and nose. Then I woke up.

Moonlight spilt through my curtains on to the bed. My sheets were drenched with sweat and twisted tight around me. My throat felt parched. I struggled to get free and as I pulled at my pillow, I heard something drop to the floor.

The key I'd found in the grandfather clock.

I got on my knees and searched around for it. While I was down there, my eye caught the dark shape under my bed. A box. The box I never look inside.

I ignored it. Tried to pretend it wasn't there. Instead, I turned the key over in my palm. I knew what I had to do. The thing I'd been avoiding for too long. I had a strong feeling that something in that room was going to help me find out about Grandad's missing memories. So why was I so scared to go in?

I put on my dressing gown and slipped my torch in the pocket. I didn't want to start turning on lights and risk waking anyone.

The house was deathly quiet. There were bars of moonlight across the landing as I crossed to the second flight of stairs. They were much narrower than the main stairs, and the wood steps were cold against my bare feet. One suddenly creaked horribly as I stood on it. I stopped, heart pounding, waiting to see if anyone had heard. Seconds ticked by. The house stayed quiet. I carried on. The stairs twisted as I climbed, my palms running up the smooth wood of the banister, and I finally found myself on the top landing, facing the forbidden door.

*Crocodiles . . . tarantulas,* a voice inside my head mocked.

My mouth felt even drier than before. I felt my skin prickle. My torch beam stretched and shrank as I stood there holding the key. Shadows scuttled under the door. I could hear the grandfather clock ticking in the downstairs hall and echoing up the walls.

*Tock, tock. . . Tock, tock. . .*

I pressed the key into the lock.

It wouldn't turn.

I used more strength, but it still didn't budge.

I pushed my shoulder against the door and tried again. This time there was a dull click. I caught my breath. I pushed the door and it opened with a weak, long whine. I looked inside.

The first thing that hit me was the smell. It was a burnt smell. The smell of ash. I wanted to leave right there and then, but I forced myself to go in.

Moonlight slanted through a triangular window at one side of the room. Strands of cobweb glistened from the ceiling and the wind whispered through a crack in the glass.

Memories from Grandad's album came back to me, things he'd told me about Grandma. I knew straightaway — this had been her room.

I slowly walked around, the floorboards shifting under my feet like the planks of a boat. Fingers of torchlight crept over her things and sent long, jagged shapes up the walls like teeth.

There was a writing desk with a framed photograph of her and her best friend, Hatty Kirby. Could that have been the string of pearls she wore on her wedding day? In one corner was a baby's cradle. Did she sit on that rocking chair with Dad on her knee?

The forbidden room was Grandma's room, all shut up. Left like a museum nobody was allowed to visit. I had the feeling of being an intruder. That I shouldn't be there. *You have no right*. I remembered Grandad's horrible reaction when he thought Lia and I had been here uninvited. *Get out. Get out!*

But I knew there had to be clues to Grandad's past somewhere. I made myself keep looking.

I touched Dad's old cradle and it creaked from side to side as if an invisible hand were rocking it. A piece of fancy material hung around its hood and I noticed that an edge of the lace was all dirty, but when I looked closer I realized that it had actually got burn marks on it.

There were other things that were wrong too. I found

burn marks on the wallpaper. In places the paper had peeled away, and underneath charred brickwork showed through. I looked up and saw that several wooden beams in the ceiling were blackened.

I felt a tingling on the back of my neck.

The fire damage, smoke damage, whatever it was, seemed worse around the window, as if that was where the fire had come from.

I began to open drawers. I felt like a thief looking for things to steal. They were all empty, except for the last one I tried, the bottom drawer of the writing desk. I found a book, about the size of my hand, damaged by strange, dark patches. DIARY was written on it in speckled gold letters. On the inside cover it said:

*Freda Smith*

I knew that diaries were supposed to be private, and I definitely didn't feel good about what I was about to do. I felt my fingers tremble. The diary came apart slightly at the spine as I turned the page and started to read.

*May 12th 1941*
*Today I told Hatty everything. About how Tommie died.*

There was a noise outside. A cold panic squeezed through me. It sounded like tree branches scraping the window, but there were no trees next to the house, not any more. Still holding the diary, I edged over and peeked out through the triangular window.

I could make out the church spire, a witch's hat against the sky. Next to it was the graveyard.

I let out a sigh of relief. Small bats were flying around outside, quick shapes in the moonlight, making high-pitched squeaks. That was what I'd heard!

The bats were darting about too fast to see properly. If only they'd settle, I thought. Stay still for a moment so I could catch a proper look at them.

Suddenly, as if it had heard me, a bat fluttered down the pane, hovering right in front of me with its delicate, paper-thin wings, before swooping away over the trees.

That's when I saw the light. Shadows rising and falling between the gravestones; a torch, like the beam of a lighthouse, a warning. For a split second it seemed to swing straight towards me.

I imagined whoever it was creeping about in the dark down there seeing my torchlight. A light in a room that nobody was supposed to go into, a room that had been shut up for years.

I flung the diary on to the writing desk, and I got out of there as fast as I could, fumbling to lock the door, scrambling down the stairs to put the key back in the clock, rushing back to my room and wrapping myself up in my ruined bed with the stone cold sheets wound tight.

# 14

# The Conchie

*The village library. Thursday, 9:23 a.m. Begging and borrowing.*

Hatty Kirby smiled at me over the library counter, and then she must have seen the look on my face because she stopped smiling.

"Whatever is the matter, Alex?"

I stood there panting and gripping a plastic bag and dripping water on to the library carpet from my saturated anorak. I'd run there all the way and my legs throbbed. I probably didn't have much time.

Dad had looked at me suspiciously at breakfast when I'd said I was popping to the library, and said he might like to come too, seeing as he'd booked today and tomorrow off work. He said that our computer at home had some sort of virus and we couldn't use it until it was fixed, so he'd come and do some reading in the library. He even invited Grandad, but he said he was too tired to go anywhere.

The truth was, Dad wanted to check up on me, I betted.

Anyway, I'd downed my toast and got out of the house as fast as I could, before he had a chance to join me.

I really wished I'd kept hold of Grandma's diary instead of getting spooked and tossing it down. I couldn't risk going back in the forbidden room during the day to read it. Someone was bound to see me. Not that I was looking forward to rifling through Grandma's private stuff, but I knew I'd have to waste a day and wait for dark before I tried again. I felt ill just thinking about going back. Something horrible had happened there. I could feel it. See it in the charred things.

Then I'd remembered Hatty. Grandma's best friend. I remembered the pictures of her in the album, the photo on Grandma's desk, what she'd said in her diary, and I figured, if anyone knew anything, Hatty Kirby would.

"I've got to talk to you," I said.

"Tell me, love."

I scanned the library. It was deserted, apart from a couple sitting by the Local History Research Room at the far end, and a woman and a little boy sitting on a beanbag in the kids' section reading a picture book.

"Grandad has to go in a home," I said. "The day after tomorrow."

Miss Kirby looked shocked. "Because of his Alzheimer's? Oh, love. I'm so sorry."

I pulled the scrapbook out of my plastic bag and put it on the counter.

"I was making him this," I said.

She leafed through. "I understand," she said. "This is a wonderful idea, Alex, it really is."

I swallowed hard. "Dad's banned me from finishing it," I said.

Miss Kirby nodded sadly. "I expect I can guess why."

"Tommie," I gasped. "I need to know. . . And about being a conchie. . . Grandad won't tell me. . . And my grandma. . . I went in her room and. . ."

I could hardly get the words out, I was so wound up.

"I want to know what happened," I told her. My hands were slapping the counter, I think, but I couldn't seem to control them. "I have to know!"

Miss Kirby pressed her hands on mine. "It's OK, love. Shhh." She glanced around and wet her lips. "Look, Alex, it's not my place to be telling you. . ."

"You have to tell me!" I heard my words pour out. My chest heaved. I felt like I was going to burst. "I need to know!" I felt my throat shudder. "It's for Grandad. I promised him. I *promised*!"

Miss Kirby nodded and laid a hand on my shoulder as I gripped the edge of the counter.

Somebody came up with a book and I put my head down, pretending to read a flier about opening times. I tried to steady my breathing. My lungs felt like they were on fire.

I heard Miss Kirby say, "Well, you know me, I should have retired years ago!" I heard her stamp a book and snap it shut, and then we were alone again.

"You might find this one interesting." She placed a small, thin book with a frayed spine on the counter and pushed it towards me. On the worn cover there was a soldier and he was crying and the title said, *The Unknown Battle of Dunkirk*.

"Thanks," I said, picking it up. I eyed the library door. "But if Dad finds out I've been asking you stuff about Dunkirk. . ."

"You can trust me not to say anything, Alex."

She sighed. "You wanted to know about your grandad being a conscientious objector. Well, a lot of people in the village were against your grandad at the time because of it."

I nodded and she went on.

"In the Second World War, people were supposed to have freedom of choice as to whether they fought, not like the First World War, when men were shot if they refused to. But there were still plenty of people ready to hand out feathers. A white feather was a symbol of a coward."

I nearly dropped the book. I remembered how Grandad had reacted in the Den when the pillow had burst open and the feathers spilt out.

"The thing was, your grandad actually did go to war," Miss Kirby said. "My guess is he probably spent more time on the front line than a lot of soldiers.

"Then his brother was killed at Dunkirk, and there were all these terrible rumours. . ."

"Did you believe them?" I interrupted her. I felt my voice rise with emotion. I was so afraid she was going to tell me the one thing I didn't want to hear. "I mean, you didn't, did you? You don't believe that Grandad could have done something like that, do you?"

She didn't seem to have heard me. Either that or she had deliberately avoided my question.

"One night your grandad was beaten up by a gang. Boys restless to get to war? A gang of ignorant lads? They never did prove who did it. But he was badly hurt. In hospital for a while. It's printed on my memory like, well, like it was yesterday. Then there were those government people hounding him. . ."

I stared. "Government people?"

She looked at me in amazement. "Don't you know anything about that?"

I shook my head. "Did Mr Webb have anything to do with all that?"

"Peter Webb? No, I don't think so. Not on that occasion. . ."

*Not on that occasion?* So was there some other occasion? I didn't have time to ask her about that, though, because I'd had a thought. The writing on the back of the photograph that Grandad had torn up. The one from the old album. The man with the cigarette between his teeth.

*Pet Vel has a smk*

What if what I'd thought had been a loopy L was really a
P, and the V a W?

## Peter Webb has a smoke

I took out the photo from the back of the scrapbook and
showed it to her.

"Yes, that's him," said Miss Kirby. "He's changed a bit,
hasn't he? He wouldn't give your grandad a minute's
peace. But I thought he'd stopped all that."

"Grandad never talked about being beaten up," I said.
"Is that how he got the scars on his hands?"

"Oh, Alex. No." She shook her head and sighed.
"Families shouldn't have secrets like that. I always
assumed you knew.

"The scars on his hands. . ." Miss Kirby trailed off. "But
surely you know the story, Alex?"

She pulled a handkerchief from her pocket and rubbed
her eyes.

"It really isn't my place to be telling you. I'd rather not
say any more."

"Please," I pleaded. "I need to know about Tommie. About
how Grandma died. You must know where she's buried."

Miss Kirby didn't reply. She picked up the date stamp
from the counter and fiddled with it. She looked past me,
and her eyebrows raised in alarm. When I turned to see
what she was looking at, I could see, through the window,
Dad and Leonard coming down the path.

Miss Kirby nodded her head towards the Research Room, and then stamped the book with a date and snapped the cover shut.

I grabbed it off the counter and bundled it into my plastic bag. Dad and Leonard were at the door, shaking the water off their umbrellas.

"Morning, Miss Kirby," Dad said. "Lovely weather we're having!"

He was still smiling when he turned to speak to me, but his voice had an edge of tension. "What's that you've got there, Alex?"

Before I could say anything, Leonard had yanked my bag out of my hand. He pulled the book out, looked at it and then held it up to Dad, smirking. I desperately tried to get a story together. Slipped in by mistake? School project? Light bedtime reading? I fumbled around with all the rubbish excuses that were racing into my head right then.

"*Fossils of the South Coast*," Leonard said with a sneer. "Sad or what?"

I snatched it back off him and stared at the cover. Instead of a soldier's face, there was an ammonite fossil on the front. I shot Miss Kirby a grateful look, but her face gave nothing away. Grandad's scrapbook was nowhere to be seen. She must have slipped it under the counter when she saw Dad outside, as well as switching books.

"So you're a boring geek now, as well as ugly!" Leonard muttered in my ear.

I tried to catch Miss Kirby's eye again, to thank her. She

looked at me, then at the book, then towards the Research Room, then back at the book, then back at me.

She did it so quickly that only I could have seen. Obviously she was trying to tell me something. Trouble is, I had no idea what.

I left Dad chatting to her and sat on a comfy chair near the newspapers. I saw Leonard glance at me from the counter and I opened the fossil book.

The due date had smudged a bit on the first page because of the speed Miss Kirby had stamped it.

**13-05-41**

Hang on!

I blinked and looked again.

**13-05-41**

The 13th of May *1941*?

I stared over at Miss Kirby. She was nodding at something Dad was saying, but she was looking straight at me.

My head whirred. The 13th of May 1941. That date, it seemed familiar.

I flicked a few pages of my fossil book and watched Dad and Leonard sit at a table with their backs to me, bent over a copy of some car magazine. Miss Kirby was busy with other customers.

I calculated what to do. I wouldn't be able to use the internet at home because of our computer being down. Lia was out with her dad all morning so I couldn't go round to hers and use it. I looked towards the Research Room. I'd have to go for that. But if one of them came in and saw what I was doing. . .

I'd have to risk it. Miss Kirby had given me a clue, and I had to follow it.

With a final glance at Dad and Leonard, I slunk out of my chair and headed for the Research Room.

I had to know what happened on the 13th of May 1941.

# 15

# May 13th 1941

*The Library Research Room. 9:37 a.m. Digging up the past.*

Our ancient village library didn't stretch to computers. Instead, the Research Room had lots of books on shelves, and a row of old-fashioned microfiche machines that you could look at newspaper reports on. You got a little piece of plastic of the date you wanted from a set of drawers and then put it in the slot and the article would be magnified on to a lit screen and you could turn a handle to scroll through it.

Despite the lack of technology, it didn't take me too long to find what I was looking for. I turned the handle, and there it was. A front-page headline from the *East Kent Herald*, dated May 13th 1941.

## TRAGIC FIRE CLAIMS LIFE

A young woman died early this morning in a dramatic blaze that has left the small community of Doverham reeling in shock.

The fire started in the early hours of the morning in an outbuilding being used as a photographic darkroom next to the house, and quickly spread to an attic bedroom and into the thatched roof.

The victim, nineteen-year-old Freda Smith, is thought to have died from smoke inhalation. Her six-month-old baby son, Richard, was rescued unharmed by her husband, William Smith.

I gasped, then kept on reading.

Mr Smith, a controversial war-photographer in the village, suffered serious burns to his hands when he attempted to enter the room and rescue his injured wife.

We tried to interview Mr Smith, but he was too distraught to comment.

I remembered Grandad's words. *"It was on fire. It was all on fire. I was on my way home. Saw the smoke. . . My Freda and the baby were in there!"*

I scrolled down fast to read more.

All Mr Smith's film and photographs were completely destroyed in the blaze.

Captain Bentley of the Dover Fire Service explained how the flames spread.

"A large tree growing close to the house caught light," he told us. "The fire then spread into the thatch. The attic room itself actually suffered only partial damage, but the victim, who is thought to have badly twisted her ankle in her hurry to get to her child, was overcome by smoke and died at the scene.

No bombers from the Channel were reported at the time and we are currently treating the blaze as suspicious.

My mind whirred. I had to read the whole thing a couple of times to let everything sink in. The article was implying the fire had been started deliberately. But by who? I scrolled through more newspaper reports but found nothing about any later trials, or anyone being charged.

As I stared at the article again, it came to me where I'd seen the date already. It was crazy that I hadn't realized before! May 13th 1941.

It was the date from the vandalized headstone.

## WINIFRED ALICE SMITH

Winifred Smith. . . Wait!

It came to me. Like a piece of a jigsaw puzzle turned this way and that way and then clicking into place.

Winifred. Wini – fred. . . Fred. Freda!

I felt my spine tingle.

The vandalized headstone.

It was the headstone of my grandma's grave.

She was killed in 1941. What had Grandad said? Grandma had married him in January. By May she was dead.

## PRIVATE SAMUEL THOMAS SMITH
## (1920–1940)

Thomas Smith . . . Tommie!

Great-Uncle Tommie must have been known by his middle name.

I heard a movement by the door of the Research Room, and in a panic spun the handle of the microfiche machine to lose the article.

I heard a voice by my shoulder. It was Miss Kirby. "We can't talk now," she said. "Your dad's looking for you."

She slipped the scrapbook into my bag, hiding it inside the fossil book, and then held out the Dunkirk book to me, her finger pointing at a name on the cover.

I opened my mouth to speak, but then the book had been whipped away again and Dad was at the door, saying, "There you are, Alex! It'll be lunchtime in awhile, and your mum and I want us all to eat together today."

But I'd had time to read the name on the Dunkirk book before Miss Kirby had hidden it. The name on the cover.

*Smith*, it had said. *Photography by W.G. Smith.*

## 16

# War Crimes

*The kitchen. Lunchtime. Water, water everywhere.*

Grandad was standing by the window when I went in, looking out at the garden, a smudge of purple under his bad eye, one finger resting against the glass as the rain streamed down. Everyone else was at the table. Mum was serving up steaming potatoes and lamb chops and green beans on to seven plates. The news droned from the little portable telly on top of the fridge.

*"The rain is set to continue. . ."*

Dad stared at it from his place. Victoria sat reading a fashion magazine. Leonard was hunched over one about cars. Sophie was dressed as a fairy and perched on a pile of cushions waving her spoon around.

All I could think about was what I'd found out at the library. Grandad rescuing Dad. Grandma's grave, the missing letters all filled in.

"Have you all washed your hands?" asked Mum. She

sounded tense. She slapped down the plates in front of us and started to cut Sophie's meat into little bits.

At some point while we ate, were we going to get told about Grandad's Big Move on Saturday? They'd have to say something soon, surely? Was that why Mum was so on edge?

When were they thinking of making their Little Family Announcement? I wondered. While we were tucking into our chops? Between the main course and pudding? Or with an after-dinner mint and a nice cup of tea?

Or was Grandad going to be whisked away to avoid a scene? Here one minute, gone the next. Done and dusted.

*"There are flood warnings across the county. . ."*

"The river will be bursting its banks by tomorrow if this keeps up," Dad muttered, picking up the salt.

*"It's raining, it's pouring, the old man is snoring,"* chanted Sophie. *"He went to bed, and bumped his head, and couldn't get up in the morning!"*

"Your father and I thought we could spend some time at the beach on Saturday morning," Mum announced cheerfully. I stared at her. "Have a nice family picnic all together."

*All together one last time, you mean.*

"Pic-nic! Pic-nic!" shrieked Sophie, dancing about.

Leonard snorted and looked at Mum like she was mad. Victoria ignored her totally and carried on reading.

I saw Mum elbow Dad.

"We've looked at the forecast," he said loudly. "More

heavy rain today and tomorrow, and then it'll be clearing up."

"What do you think, Alex?" Mum looked at me. There was a sort of pleading look in her eyes.

I shrugged and speared a green bean with my fork. I wasn't going to say anything to help ease her guilt complex. I wished that they'd just come out and tell us if they were going to. Get it over with.

But if they didn't say anything? I leaned over to put some butter on to Grandad's potatoes. I willed him to sit down and start to eat. If only we could get through lunch without them saying anything. I could still have time to finish the scrapbook. I could still have time to change their minds.

If Leonard hadn't grassed on me and Grandad by now, maybe he never would.

*Eat!* I shouted in my head. *Take a bite, for God's sake!*

Grandad came away from the window and stood over the kettle. "Who wants tea?" he asked.

"No, thanks," chorused Mum and Dad.

"*I* will, thanks," I said.

"Who'll play with me after?" piped Sophie.

"Off you go, Alex!" taunted Leonard. He made a gun with his hand in his lap and pulled the trigger at me. "Go play with my baby sister."

"Who wants tea?" asked Grandad again.

Leonard did an over-the-top sigh.

"No, thanks, William," said Mum mechanically.

"I will, Grandad," I said. "Thanks."

"Who'll play? Who'll play?" pestered Sophie. She sounded as if she was going to go into a tantrum any minute. Dad flicked the volume of the telly up a bar with the remote control.

*"There are already reports of dangerously high river levels. . ."*

I watched Grandad sit down and stare at his plate. I thought about all the things in his life he'd been through that I'd known nothing about. Why hadn't he told me about the Dunkirk book? Why had he never shown me Grandma's grave?

Grandad picked up his fork.

Then his knife.

He sawed at a piece of meat and ate it.

I looked at Dad. He couldn't even know who'd saved him from the fire when he was a baby. You only had to look at the way he treated Grandad to tell that.

I looked at Mum and Victoria, even Sophie, and I thought to myself, they should all know the truth about Grandad. They ought to know.

Grandad chewed a potato.

Except I didn't know the truth, did I? Not the whole of it. I didn't know how Tommie died and whether Grandad was really to blame. If he had been, well, maybe it didn't matter how many other good things he'd done in his life. That would be the thing he was remembered for.

Grandad gathered up a forkful of green beans.

He'd cleared half his plate.

So far so good.

I ate faster, hardly tasting my food, intent on getting finished and getting away from that table without a scene, and inviting Lia round, and telling her what I'd found out. . .

And that's what might have happened next.

If Leonard hadn't gone and opened his big mouth.

"*The Ministry of Defence today announced pay rises for the armed forces. . .*" blared the telly.

"Pass the parsley, darling," Mum said.

"Must be short of soldiers," muttered Grandad. "I'd have thought there were more than enough."

"You can never have enough soldiers," said Leonard.

"Can't you?" Grandad stabbed a fork into his chop.

Leonard swamped his plate with gravy. "Well, *I'm* joining up as soon as I'm sixteen!"

A silence hung over the table with the steam from the potatoes.

"As if!" snorted Victoria at last. "You'll never pass the physical!"

I saw that Grandad had stopped chewing. He had gone very still. He had a corner of tablecloth clenched in one fist.

I gripped my knife and fork. The only thing I'd wanted was for us to get through lunch in peace. Why couldn't Leonard have stayed upstairs playing his stupid war games? Why did he have to bring them to the table instead?

"When I join the army. . ." he began.

153

Grandad cut him off. "You won't be."

Leonard stared at him with a scowl. "What?"

"Joining up."

"Says who?"

"I said you won't be. That's an end to it."

"It's my life," said Leonard. "You can't stop me."

Grandad pushed his chair back from the table. "I don't believe in war," he said. "Never have and never will. There're plenty of other ways to solve problems. I've been on a battlefield, and there's no glory in it, I can ruddy well tell you that now, Leonard. It's not like one of your computer games."

"What place is it of yours to say what he will and won't do?" cut in Dad. "I'm his father."

We all turned to look at him.

"More green beans, anyone?" piped Mum.

Grandad leaned towards Dad. His voice starting to crack with anger.

"You want him to be a soldier, do you? You want that? Your own son? Killing people? Getting killed himself?"

"He should be allowed to make his own decisions, that's all I'm saying."

"Like I did, you mean?" Grandad said.

Mum started spooning great heaps of extra green beans on to everyone's plates. Victoria had sunk down in her seat, trying to stay well out of it. Sophie stared from Grandad to Dad and back again with an interested look on her face.

"Some people can only make selfish decisions," said Dad.

Grandad got to his feet. A knife clattered to the floor.

"That's what you think I was, do you, Richard? Selfish!"

Dad banged a hand on the table. "We damn well should fight! If our way of life is threatened. If our families are threatened."

"Don't judge things you know nothing about."

Dad rose slightly from his seat. "I know something! I know that you came back but Tommie didn't."

"Richard!" Green beans flew from Mum's spoon.

"So that's what this is all about, is it?" I'd never seen Grandad look so angry. "Mildred really did work well on you, Richard, didn't she?"

So Lia's idea was right. Great Aunt Mildred had been saying bad things to Dad about Grandad while he was growing up.

Mum slapped an extra lamb chop on to Dad's plate. But he was on a roll.

"You know what you were, William?" he said. His voice trembled and his face had gone a funny colour. He spat out the word. "You were a *coward*."

He said it like he'd been wanting to the whole of his life, like it had been trapped inside him all this time and it was a relief to let it out at last. To finally say what he'd been wanting to say all along, and not care who was listening. He even seemed to give a laugh as he said it.

"Richard, that's enough!"

Dad glanced at Mum and then pulled the newspaper up in front of his face with a grunt.

Grandad looked like he wanted to say more. But then he saw Sophie gawping at him and instead he yanked open the patio door and strode away into the rain and down the garden towards the Den.

I felt like running after him, but I figured he didn't want company right then.

"I've work to do," said Dad, throwing down the paper and going off in the other direction.

Mum heaved the patio door shut. "I've got work to do as well," she snapped, starting to clear the plates. "All of you, out of my kitchen!"

"But what about pudding?" protested Leonard. "I'm not even finished!"

"Out, I said. Now!"

So much for the Little Family Announcement.

Maybe I should have felt grateful to Leonard. But all I felt was numb.

We filed out of the kitchen and went into the lounge.

"Tick, tock," taunted Leonard as he leaned over me to look for the remote control. "Tick, tock."

I pushed him away.

"Face the truth, Bosnia Boy. I heard Mum and Dad talking. Grandad's time's up, and yours is too."

"Well done for starting off that lovely argument, Leonard!" Victoria sprawled along the settee with the remote control and flicked on the television. Sophie started pulling jigsaw pieces from a toy box in the corner. The tail end of the news came on. Some item about a man on trial. . .

"What's on the other side?" said Leonard, flopping down in Grandad's armchair. "Turn off this boring rubbish, can't you?"

"Some of us like to keep in touch with the planet we live in," said Victoria.

"Which planet would that be in your case, Vickie dear?"

I watched Sophie slap the jigsaw pieces in. She couldn't get any to fit. She kept turning them and trying to force them in, but nothing worked. In the end she gave up and started wiggling a piece of wool across the carpet.

"Naughty, Moggy! Play with me. Don't scratch the furniture!"

"*The war crimes trial. . . Bosnia. . .*"

That was all I needed. I saw Victoria glance at me.

A picture came up on the screen. An old man with a beard and glasses.

"You can't imagine an old man like that doing murder and stuff," said Victoria. "He looks like somebody's grandad!"

"We're missing the start of *Combat Unit*!" complained Leonard.

Victoria sighed and threw him the remote. "There you go, moron." She started leafing through a fashion magazine.

That was it.

Leonard changed channel and the screen was filled with blokes firing paint at each other and killing themselves laughing.

Mum came in and started plumping cushions around us, slapping them a lot harder than she needed to. Sophie sat chatting to a one-armed doll.

Everyone carrying on as normal.

As if nothing whatsoever had happened.

# 17

# Playing With Fire

*In the lounge. 2:45 p.m. Two heads better than one.*

"They seem to have the totally wrong idea about your grandad."

Lia had come round and we had the lounge to ourselves. The others had driven to the shopping mall in Dover. Grandad still hadn't come out of the Den.

"He saved your dad from a burning house, but your dad thinks he's a coward! And he may have been a conchie, but we know he had a hard time of it, being beaten up and all that." She stroked the hair of Sophie's doll. "What I don't understand is, why didn't your grandad just tell your dad what really happened?"

"Maybe it was too hard for him to talk about," I said. "I mean, Dad was saved but my grandma died. Maybe it was easier for him never to say anything about it."

"Hmmm." Lia looked at me doubtfully. "Well, I agree with you. I think your family need to know what happened." She clicked her fingers. "I know! You can tell them all straight when you're together. Show them the scrapbook. Tell them everything you know! I reckon it might be the only way to get your dad to listen."

"OK," I said slowly. "Mum wants us all to have a picnic on the beach on Saturday morning. . ."

"Perfect!" said Lia. "You can do it then."

"But not unless we've got all the parts worked out," I said.

"Like what happened to Tommie, you mean?"

"You don't think Grandad had anything to do with it, do you?" I said. I felt queasy just thinking about it. I wanted Lia to say, "Course not, Alex. Don't be an idiot!" But how could she know? How could either of us know for sure?

Imagine it. Imagine that you find out that your grandad did things when he was younger. Terrible things that nobody will speak about.

"You've got to go back up there."

I stared at Lia.

"To your grandma's room." She wheeled herself across the room and picked up one of Sophie's jigsaw pieces. "Tonight. Read the rest of the diary."

I felt myself go tense.

"You can't go up there now, can you? And you can't bring it down here! Your grandad might come in any minute. I think you need to wait until everyone's in bed again. Get the key out of the clock and go back. Surely you were planning to do that anyway?"

Yes, I was, but the thought of being up there in the dark again, alone. . .

"I'd come with you," said Lia. She gave me a punch on the arm. "But I'm not too good with steps, am I?"

# 18

# Grandma's Diary

*In Grandma's room. Half-past midnight. Scared out of my wits.*

The diary wasn't where I'd left it.

If I could have got out of there right then, I would have done, but my feet were rooted to the floorboards. I was paralysed.

*You have to keep looking, Alex*, I told myself. *It's for your grandad.*

The diary wasn't on top of the writing desk, where I thought I'd thrown it. It was back in the drawer.

My memory was playing tricks on me, I told myself. Really I had put it back; I'd been scared by the torchlight in the graveyard and wasn't thinking straight.

I tried to stay calm. I crouched with the diary, and then opened the front cover, letting the light from my torch spill over the pages as I turned them.

*May 12th 1941*

A shudder rippled through me. She'd written it the day before she died.

*Today I told Hatty everything. About how Tommie died.*

It was difficult to read. My torch shone over the closely spaced, curling handwriting. Here and there were dark lines of smoke damage like scars.

*I'm writing all this down so it won't be lost. The only sure way to remember things is to write them down. Tommie's death taught me that. You need to remember things. Keep your secrets safe. And every family has its secrets. Ours more than most.*

*I know what people are saying. But William says let them talk. They have to come to the truth themselves, not have it rammed down their throats. I hate their lies, but I agree with William. Even if we told them the truth, would they believe it? People believe what they want to.*

*William wouldn't tell me what really happened to Tommie. Not for a long time. His heart was too broken. When he finally did tell me I had no doubt it was the truth because William could never lie to me. I would know it.*

*That day in May last year. So many were saved,*

but so many died too. We heard the call for boats to rescue the soldiers off the Dunkirk beaches. William started getting a boat ready as soon as he found out, and there was nothing anybody could have said to him to make him change his stubborn, brave mind.

Tommie was on leave at the time. He'd had a bad wound to the leg and wasn't allowed to fly, although it was nearly healed. He insisted that he went with William. William wouldn't hear of it. But Tommie kept on and on until William gave in. I was feeling too sick to argue with them. I wish to God that I had.

Tommie was so proud of his brother! He admired the way that he stood firm with his pacifist principles. He was so proud of Will's photographs too. He said that the world had to see them because they told the truth about war. That war has to be avoided at all costs.

So, that day in May they set off in Will's boat...

There were smoke marks on the page, making it impossible to read in places.

...Tommie got trapped on the beach...
...William tried to...

I held the torch closer to the page, desperate to make out the words.

*. . .William tried to save Tommie. . .*

I read that line again and again.

*William tried to save Tommie.*

*William tried to save Tommie!*

I felt like leaping about yelling, thumping the air with my fist. Grandad had tried to save his brother! Grandad had tried to save his brother!

But then I read the next bit and I felt a coldness creep over me.

*I'm afraid.*

*Peter Webb has been making threats. He's more and more unbalanced since his brother Henry's death. He won't listen to reason. He hates the photographs Will took. He stormed into Will's darkroom today while Will was working and tried to destroy a roll of film he had.*

*I am tired now, and Richard needs feeding. Will has been so good as a father to him. I don't know what I would have done without him. I hope he will be home soon. He has been helping Hatty's father with some fences and is due back late.*

I closed the diary and held it against me. It was the last thing my grandma had ever written. By the next morning she was dead.

If only she'd known what was going to happen. She

could have changed things. Things would have turned out so differently.

I hugged the book close, and then slipped it in my dressing gown pocket. I would show it to Dad and he would read his mum's words and he would finally know the truth. Not Great-Aunt Mildred's truth, or Mr Webb's, but the real truth.

As I went out, I stumbled. My foot must have caught on the bottom of my pyjamas. I went sprawling, my torch clattered down and went out, and as I put a hand out to break my fall, I heard something spin away from it. I scrambled around in the dark and my fingers touched something cold and round.

Somehow I got my torch on again and looked at what I'd found. It must have been hidden under the writing desk.

It was a metal box. A canister. About the size of a saucer. Badly dented and blackened. I turned it over. Words were printed on it.

## PHOTOGRAPHIC FILM

My heart started thumping wildly. Could it be what I thought it was?

What if all Grandad's photographs and films hadn't been destroyed by the fire? Could a film have survived somehow?

## OPEN ONLY IN THE DARK

My head was beaded with sweat. If I had opened the canister, even in the torchlight, I'd have ruined the film inside. I knew that much. Grandad was a good photography teacher.

There was other writing on the canister. I recognized Grandad's scrawl.

The only one saved.

Then, in even smaller writing, the letters all messy as if his hand was trembling at the time:

1940
1940, Dunkirk.

# 19

# Some Things Best Forgotten

*The vicarage. Friday, 8:50 a.m. Religious intervention.*

The church lawns were more swamp than grass and my trainers were filthy by the time I reached Reverend Posselthwaite's front door.

"I wondered when you'd call, Alex!" he said, as soon as he saw me. "Yes, I have it!"

I knew he meant the rubbing from Grandma's gravestone, but that wasn't the only thing I'd come for. I was pretty sure by now what the missing letters were on the inscription, and I was pretty sure who'd hacked them out.

It was Peter Webb I wanted to talk to the vicar about.

I started to take my shoes off, but Reverend Posselthwaite hurried me into his study. He seemed oblivious to the big dirty footprints I was leaving on Mrs Posselthwaite's cream carpet.

Mr Webb was one of the final pieces of the story I needed, I was sure of it. The piece I needed to back up

Grandma's diary and prove Grandad's bravery. Once I had that, I thought nervously, I would try and develop the film.

Hope shot through me. Tomorrow they were supposed to be taking Grandad away. But by tomorrow I'd have everything I needed.

Reverend Posselthwaite rummaged through the pile of cardboard tubes and rolled-up paper on his desk. "I had it only a moment ago. . ." he said. "Your grandma was actually *Winifred*, don't you know? Luckily both names were written on the tube. But then I got sidetracked. I had to go and sort out the flowers in the church. Now that poor Peter Webb is sadly no longer with us. . ."

I gaped at him. "Mr Webb?"

"Yes." The vicar stopped and pushed up his glasses. "Didn't you hear? Oh, I'm sorry if I shocked you with the news. He died this morning."

I stood there, stunned.

"He did great service for our church," the vicar went on. "He put flowers on the altar every day, and helped keep the graveyard tidy. He wasn't a well man. He'd been ill for some time. I gather he wasn't the easiest of people to get to know, but he had time to make his peace before he died. I heard his last confession and we prayed together."

*Last confession?*

I took a deep breath.

"Did Peter Webb start the fire? The one that killed my grandma?"

I felt guilty, with him having just died and all that, but I had to know for sure. The newspaper article had said the fire had been started on purpose. Grandma had said she was scared at what Mr Webb might do next.

The vicar stared at me, then looked down. "Alex. Alex." He took off his glasses and polished them on his sleeve. "That's not for me to repeat."

"She was my grandma," I said. "I've a right to know. So has Grandad."

He looked at me with a sad, kind expression. "It's tomorrow afternoon, isn't it? That he moves to the Sunflower Care Home?"

So even the vicar knew about it before Grandad did! But then I remembered Mum's tense conversation with Mrs Posselthwaite on the day of the fête, so I suppose that made sense.

The vicar sat there for a while, rubbing his glasses so hard I thought he'd go right through the lens any minute. He went to a drawer, took out an envelope and handed it to me.

"Peter Webb gave me this," he said. "Only yesterday."

I looked at the words on the front.

*To Richard Smith and family*

"It's addressed mainly to your dad, as you can see. But all your family, actually, so I think it's right that you can take it."

He saw me hesitating. "Open it, Alex. Peter asked me to read it to him before I put it in the envelope, so I know what it says. He wouldn't settle until I did. Open it!"

I turned the envelope over a few times and then slowly tore it open. There was a single piece of paper in there. It was thin and flimsy. I pulled it out, unfolded it and began reading. I guess my bad opinion of Mr Webb changed a bit as I read that letter.

*It was me what set fire to William Smith's darkroom. It were the photos I was after. I never meant for it to spread and I never meant for her to die. Losing someone close is just about the worst thing can happen to a person. I should know. You lose a piece of yourself. I know you were only a baby, but it weren't right. Anyway, I'm sorry for it, that you lost your mother on account of what I done. I hope you can think to forgive me because I never can.*

*Peter Webb*

"Peter Webb lost his older brother Henry in the war," said the vicar quietly. "He absolutely idolized his brother. He'd never been allowed to join up himself, because of the bad limp he had, and his bad back. From a childhood disease it was, nothing to do with fighting. I don't think he ever came to terms with Henry getting killed, poor man. I don't think he ever recovered from it. I think it affected his mind. He even went round wearing his brother's medals.

"Grief, Alex. Grief is a terrible thing."

Reverend Posselthwaite stared out of the window at the rain. "He was very sorry at the end, I think. For everything. Genuinely sorry."

I stared down at the letter and nodded. The words seemed to go a bit blurry and I quickly rubbed my eyes and put the paper back in the envelope and in my pocket.

Peter Webb's secret. His terrible secret.

At the door of the porch, Reverend Posselthwaite stopped a moment and touched my arm. "Wait!" He disappeared back down the hallway and came back with a rolled sheet of paper.

I'd almost forgotten. The inscription!

I waited, expecting the reverend to tell me how Peter Webb had admitted to vandalizing the headstone, and that he was sorry for that too. . .

But Reverend Posselthwaite just wrapped a plastic carrier bag around the rubbing and smiled at me encouragingly. If Peter Webb had chiselled away the letters, he would have wanted to say something about that too, surely?

I didn't have time to think about that then, though. I made sure the bag was sealed tight. All I had to do now was put the rubbing against the inscription on the headstone. Check what the missing letters were.

My heart raced. I could stop them sending Grandad

172

into the home! I really could! Once Mum and Dad knew the whole truth about Grandad's past, things would be different. They would want to keep him with us; they'd want us to stay all together as a family, not split us up.

I pulled up the hood of my anorak and headed into the graveyard.

# PART 3

# GRAND FINALES

# 20

# Red Carnations

*The graveyard. Twenty minutes later. The moment of truth.*

I knelt by Grandma's gravestone and unrolled the paper against the dull marble. The tree branches overhead gave some shelter from the rain, though some water splashed off the paper's waxy surface. The vase of red carnations was still there, the petals slightly tinged in brown.

The letters fitted exactly, and I read through the inscription, filling in the missing parts.

WINIFRED ALICE SMITH
BORN 1922
DIED 13TH OF MAY 1941
LOST TO US BEFORE HER TIME
FOUND BY OUR CREATOR
KILLED BY FIRE, NOW LIVING IN LIGHT

I knew that much.

BELOVED WIFE OF
PRIVATE SAMUEL THOMAS SMITH
(1920–1940)
AND
WILLIAM GEORGE SMITH

So far so good. It confirmed everything I already knew.

But that wasn't all there was. There was more inscription on the rubbing. I smoothed the paper and stared at what was written in disbelief, and then I started pulling and scraping at the thick ivy growing around the bottom of the stone. Soil clogged my fingernails as I tugged the twisting stalks and roots away.

It couldn't be. But when I'd finished, what was on the rubbing was an exact copy of the overgrown words I'd uncovered.

**BELOVED MOTHER OF**
**RICHARD SMITH**
**NOW BOTH HIS PARENTS WALK**
**WITH ANGELS**

*Both* his parents?

I stood there with rain dripping down my face, trying to take it in.

The words in Grandma's diary came back to me.

*Will has been so good as a father to him. I don't
know what I would have done without him.*

Dad was Tommie's son, not Grandad's.

Grandad was Dad's uncle.

"So now you know, Alex."

I twisted round.

Grandad was standing there. Rain dripped off the brim
of his hat.

"Your dad already knows," he said. "I'd never have kept
something like that a secret from him. He always knew
who his real father was."

Grandad stooped and pulled the dying carnations from
the vase.

"Always preferred Freda to Winifred, your grandma
did," he said. "But somehow Mildred got her own way on
that one. Said it was only proper to use the name she was
baptized under, and at the time I wasn't in much of a fit
state to argue."

He pulled a fresh bunch of carnations from his pocket
and eased them into the vase.

"I come out here at night sometimes," he said. "When I
can't sleep so well. It sounds silly, but I want to be alone
with her; not have to worry about anyone else being
about."

Raindrops collected on the petals. Of course it was
Grandad bringing the flowers, I thought. Of course he
would visit Grandma's grave! I remembered the torchlight

I'd seen from Grandma's room. He probably went up there too. It was he who must have put the diary back. He who kept the key safe in the clock.

I watched him rest his hand on the top of the stone. Questions spun around inside my head. "Why didn't Dad or you ever tell us that Tommie was our real grandad?" I stammered.

Grandad fingered the wet collar of his coat.

"I can't speak for your dad, why he didn't tell you, but me. . ." He hung his head. "I suppose I always wanted to be your real grandad, and when your mum and dad never said anything. . ."

A memory came back to me. Me and Grandad in the beer garden the day of the church fête when I told him Leonard wasn't my real brother. The hurt look on his face when he said, *I'm not your real grandad then, am I?*

When Grandad had talked about bad blood in the family, I realized now, he'd not meant Leonard; he'd not meant Dad.

He'd meant himself.

"I'm a fraud, Alex, see?" he said, his voice shaking. "I'm not your real grandad after all."

"Course you are!" I said. "Don't talk like that! But you could have shown me Grandma's grave. Why didn't you?"

Grandad shrugged. "Too many memories," he struggled. "Having to explain to other people. . ." He fingered the vandalized inscription.

"I wish I'd not taken the letters out. . ."

I gasped. "What?"

He ran his thumb along where his name should have been. "I regretted it later but, well, I wasn't in a good place at the time, Alex. I wasn't right, you know, mentally. I just couldn't come to terms with how Freda died, and somehow. . ." He swallowed.

I stood there.

## WILLIAM GEORGE SMITH

I thought about the letters being chipped away bit by bit, carefully, almost lovingly.

Peter Webb hadn't done it.

Grandad had.

"It sounds crazy now," he went on. "But at the time it seemed I was somehow, I don't know . . . intruding on the two of them, having my name there too.

"And then over time the stone started to slant at this funny angle. Ground subsidence, it must have been."

I put my hand on Grandad's. "Tell me about Tommie," I said. "Please."

He started to shake his head.

"Please, Grandad. I have to know."

Grandad looked up at the sky through the branches. A flock of birds swept across a patch of grey. Rain ran down his face. He drew in a breath, long and slow.

"The fighter planes kept coming," he said. His voice

was all husky, as if it hurt him to speak. "There were dozens of them. One after the other. Another and another. You didn't have a clue who'd be hit next."

I felt his cold hand tremble in mine. "Bodies on the beach, there were. Bodies in the water. . . Gone, they were. Wiped out. . .

"Tommie was shouting at me, *'Keep shooting, Will! You've got to keep shooting!'*

"Another enemy plane came over, making a low swoop. It had these sirens on the wings, and I'll never forget the way it sounded." Grandad screwed up his face. "It was this deafening, screeching, wailing horror of a sound, and I was still shooting pictures but then I saw that the plane was coming straight at us and I jumped at Tommie and pushed him away and the line of bullets hit the sand just where he'd been."

Grandad let out a sob through his gritted teeth. "At first I thought we'd got away with it. But then I saw there was blood in Tommie's mouth. . . I saw there were pieces of jagged metal beside us. Bits from a blown-up jeep. I'd not seen them there." I felt Grandad's fingernails dig into my hand. "I'd pushed Tommie straight on to one."

He covered his mouth and gave out a strange, shuddering whimper.

"He knew he wasn't going to make it. He'd lost too much blood. I was pressing his chest where the metal had gone in. I was crouched over him and I was pressing as hard as I could. Pressing, pressing. . ."

Grandad lifted up his hands and stared at them. Rain splashed on his palms and trickled down his sleeves.

"Tommie was looking at his blood coming through my fingers, and he seemed to sort of laugh at me, and said, 'Don't be daft, Will.'

"He said, 'Promise me, Will. Promise me you'll look after my Freda. Marry her. Look after her and the little one.' He knew I loved her too, you see.

"He had hold of the collar of my jacket and I had to bend right low to hear what he was saying. I remember the blood on his teeth. A gurgling sound in his chest when he breathed. 'Leave me here. Get yourself out. Show them what it's all really like, all this fighting, all this ruddy killing. You promise me, Will?' And I said yes and then he sort of twisted up and he looked so sad and afraid and lonely. . ." Grandad swayed and tears ran down his face. ". . .I wanted to die there with him.

"He shouted out a single word. His last. Her name."
*Freda.*

I wanted to cry like Grandad was. I wanted to screw up my face and let the tears stream down like he was doing, but I couldn't. I rocked myself forward and back. Forward and back. What was wrong with me? Why couldn't I cry?

I hugged Grandad as he sobbed, and when we were standing quietly again, I asked, "Why is Great-Aunt Mildred so against you?"

His bruised, wet eyelid glistened. "Mildred was engaged to Henry Webb, as you know. He died the same year, a bit later on, though. He was saved from Dunkirk. A navy ship brought him out. He'd seen what happened with me and Tommie and he'd told Mildred about it."

He stroked the carnation petals.

"When Henry was killed, she started telling people her own twisted version of the story. That I deliberately pushed Tommie to kill him. So somehow your dad got the wrong end of the stick."

"But why would Aunt Mildred do that?"

Grandad shook his head. "It's hard to know exactly. Maybe she thought all her hopes for the future had been snatched away when Henry died. When she saw Freda and me get together, she felt, well, bitter, I suppose."

The vicar's words came back to me. *Grief, Alex. Grief is a terrible thing.*

"Even after your grandma was gone, she stuck to her story," said Grandad. "She probably believed it by then, anyway."

"But why didn't you tell Dad the truth?" I said. "You should have told him. You just told me!"

"I tried. . ." Grandad sighed. "I wanted to. But. . . But it was difficult, Alex. Going over it all again. You of all people know that!"

He hunched his shoulders. "Your dad was right. I am a coward. I didn't want to admit I'd pushed Tommie on to that metal."

"But it was an accident, Grandad! You saved him from the bullets!"

184

Grandad looked down at Grandma's grave. "First Tommie," he said. "Then my Freda."

I buried my face in Grandad's chest, feeling it heave under me, feeling his heart thumping, hard and strong.

"Do you know Peter Webb's dead?" I said, but he didn't seem to have heard me.

"I promised Tommie I'd develop my films," he said. "Show them to everyone who'd look. I managed to get a small book out pretty quick with a few of the first pictures I developed. Self-published, it was. But all the copies and all the negatives were destroyed when the darkroom went up. There was one roll left after the fire. God knows how it survived. I always meant to develop it, after what I promised Tommie. . . But I hadn't the heart to, not after Freda died. I couldn't do it."

"Hatty Kirby has a copy of the book, Grandad, and . . ." I swallowed. ". . . I found the film. In Grandma's room. I'm sorry I went in there. I shouldn't have done, but I had to. . ."

Grandad shuddered. "Don't ask me to develop it," he pleaded. "I don't want to look at those photos." He started rifling round in his pocket and pulled out the key to the Den. He forced it into my hand. "I couldn't face looking at them. Don't make me."

"I won't ask you to. Shhh. . . It's OK."

Grandad clutched my arm, like Sophie might when she was scared.

Seeing him made me remember the look in my babo's eyes. . .

*Focus on Grandad*, I told myself.

"I know about the Sunflower," he said suddenly. "Your mum and dad told me, a bit back.

"I don't want to go, Alex."

He pulled at his beard and looked around, as if he didn't recognize anything. "I can't remember how to get home," he whimpered. "Help me find my way home."

I squeezed his arm and nodded, and as I led him back through the graveyard I knew that I needed those photographs for the scrapbook. I needed them for Dad. He had to see them. I had to develop that film as soon as I could.

There was only one problem.

One big problem.

I would have to do it without Grandad.

But I wasn't sure I could remember how.

# 21

## The Front Line

*In Grandad's darkroom. 10:29 a.m. No room for error.*

When we got back, Mum made Grandad change into dry clothes and put his feet up, and then she and Dad went out shopping. They'd wanted to drag Grandad with them, but they must have seen he wasn't up to it. They wanted to treat him to some new things, Mum said. I waited while she droned through the list: *A new pair of pyjamas, slippers, a nice new cardigan. . . And there are hummus and cucumber sandwiches in the fridge and chocolate cake for lunch in case we're late back. . .* All I could think about were the photographs, the film I had to develop.

What if I messed up? If I got something wrong, the whole film could be ruined and the last ever pictures Grandad took at Dunkirk, the only surviving film, would be lost for ever.

Victoria was left on Sophie duty and they went to watch telly in the lounge with Grandad. Leonard went off to his room with a wedge of cake. I waited for the car to reverse down the drive and then I was under the dining table and on the phone to Lia. Luckily she was in, and when she heard what I had to do, she said she'd be straight round.

I slipped to the Den with the film canister and locked the door behind me.

Nothing was where it should be. Mum had quickly tidied around the place from after the darkroom got messed up, but I spent ages searching for the right bottles of chemicals in the backs of cupboards and checking all the equipment was there. I'd just finished laying the last tray along the darkroom bench when there was a soft knock on the door and I let Lia in.

"Right." Lia looked along the bench. "Just one more time. What do you need to do again?"

It was the fifth time she had made me talk her through the developing process and it was a good job she did because I started getting confused about what to do and when. I was too nervous. I couldn't think straight. Grandad had always been on hand before to remind me. I knew I had to get everything right. The mix of chemicals, the timing, the temperatures. . . Everything had to be done in exactly the right order too, or I was in trouble.

After all these years, would the images still be there? Would the film even be any good, after getting a cooking in the fire?

Lia looked at me from under her fringe. "You can do it,

Alex. Take your time. Try and remember exactly what you did when you helped your grandad."

I nodded at her, blew a quick breath out and I started.

I laid the canister on the bench and pulled down the blackout blinds, blotting out the gloomy light outside. . .

. . . And don't ask me how, I hardly knew myself, but a while later a curling plastic strip was hanging on the drying rack.

I had the negatives. And most of them looked OK, like they really could be OK.

I switched on the red light. I thought of Grandad. I thought of what the pictures could prove about him. The part of his life that they could give him back.

. . . I used tongs to lay a piece of printing paper in the developing tray. My hands were so unsteady that some of the liquid inside splashed out. I held the tray more firmly and tipped the whole thing, letting the chemical solution slide over the surface of the paper. I rocked the tray backwards and forwards and an image appeared from the red skin of liquid. I dipped it in the tray of fixer while Lia worked the timer and checked the temperatures of the chemicals, and then I rinsed the photo under the tap and pegged it on the drying line.

The paper quivered, dripping water on to the bench like spots of blood.

Lia and I stared at each other, not saying anything.

I wanted to stop right then. I wanted to get out of that room. But I felt Lia's hand grip my shoulder and somehow I was able to keep concentrating on what I had to do.

So I went on like some kind of robot, not wanting to look at what was in those trays, not wanting to think about them. We hung up photo after photo. I'd no idea how long it took. Black-and-white photo after black-and-white photo. On and on until we'd done them all. There were dozens of them, rectangular pieces of paper clipped with little pegs, like gravestones standing in a line.

When Grandad said Tommie had told him to keep shooting, now I knew exactly what he had meant.

I'll never forget the faces. The dirty, desperate faces of those soldiers. One sat with his hands wrapped over his head; another was slumped and crying. Another was cowering and clutching a photo of a baby. Men scrambling on to boats while planes swooped overhead, the water splashing up as the bullets hit. Broken ships on fire, sending black plumes into the sky.

There was plenty of death, plenty of bodies, bodies lying, floating. Bodies twisted up into strange shapes, black stains around them on the beach.

No wonder Peter Webb wanted to burn the films. Who wanted to see their dead brother, or their son, or their father lying there like that? They'd want a statue instead, with *"Our Finest Hour"* chiselled into a stone scroll. They'd want flags draped over coffins and bugle salutes.

Grandad did shoot people. He did fight.

He shot photographs. He fought for the truth.

The truth about war. The truth about the terrible things people did to one another.

And Dad thought he was a coward.

But now I was ready to tell him and my whole family the truth, and seeing those photos I knew that when I did, there'd be no more talk about the Sunflower Care Home. There'd be no more talk about sending Grandad away anywhere.

From the way she was looking at me, I think Lia must have understood too.

I'd be able to keep my promise to Grandad.

I stared at the last photo hanging there.

The very last picture from the roll of film.

A man, pointing up, mouth frozen in a shout.

Behind him in the sky . . . the blur of a plane. Too low, too fast. . .

It was a face I knew.

It was Tommie.

I tugged at a blackout blind and it swept upwards with a snap. I opened the window, filling my lungs with the smell of wet summer grass. The rain had stopped. It felt like I had resurfaced after being underwater.

I stood there a while and then closed the window.

The scrapbook was almost ready. But there was something I still wanted to do. Somebody I wanted to show the photos to first. A few last details I needed to check.

Something made me jump back.

There was a face mouthing against the glass.

Leonard.

He was pointing down the garden and he was shouting something, screaming something about the river . . . about Grandad.

I rushed out and he came at me and gripped my arms, hurting them.

"We kept telling him not to," he gasped. "But he wouldn't listen."

Fear shot through me.

"The river's nearly burst its banks," Leonard panted. "Grandad's in the boat. Victoria told him the water was too fast and deep, but he wouldn't. . ."

I broke into a run.

I heard Leonard cry out behind me.

"Sophie's in the boat too."

# 22

# Dunkirk

*The bottom of the garden. 2:40 p.m. Messing about on the river.*

"We have to save our boys!" Grandad shouted when he saw me.

He had a wild look. The boat was right out in the middle of the river, swaying badly. He stooped, struggling to untie the end of rope attached to the *Little Swift*.

Sophie stood at one end of the juddering hull. She waved happily. "Alex!"

"Sit down, Sophie!" Victoria screeched from the bank.

I paced the edge, my fingers covering my mouth. . .

"She jumped on before we could stop her," Leonard panted behind me. "She thought it was a game."

. . . I clasped my hands behind my head. My palms squeezed the back of my skull.

"Sit down, Sophie!" Lia bellowed. She was close to the river, stuck fast in mud, desperately trying to get the wheels of her chair to turn. "Keep still!"

"Come on!" Sophie stretched out a chubby hand and the boat rocked violently. "We're going on an adventure to save the soldiers! Me and Grandad and Moggy!"

"Sophie can't swim, Grandad!" Victoria shouted at him, but he didn't seem to be able to take in what she was saying. He went on tugging the knot.

The long rope lashed the water. Its other end was fastened around one of the willow trees on the bank, and the loop jarred from side to side, rubbing the bark raw.

I stared as the thudding water splashed the trunks. I thought about Grandad's burnt pillow I'd buried there. That dark scorch like an open sore. A war wound.

"She's got no life jacket on, Grandad." I slipped on the bank, sending lumps crumbling into the churning water. I slammed down on my back and rolled in the dirt, nearly going over myself. I scrambled up. "She can't swim!"

Grandad fumbled with the knot. "We've got to get our boys out."

It was as if he didn't see Sophie. He didn't even seem to realize that she was on the boat with him. He was completely in his own world. Trapped in his own past.

The swollen river looked like it was boiling.

"Tommie is out there somewhere!" he cried. "I've got to get to Dunkirk and find him!"

"He thinks he's back in nineteen forty," Lia yelled at me.

"The war's over, Grandad!"

"Stay there, Sophie!" Victoria screamed. "You've got to

194

sit down!" She slipped on the mud and fell. "Ow!" She got up and then sat down again, clutching her ankle, her face screwed up in pain. "Do something, Leonard!" she shrieked.

Leonard stared at the water, his face white as a sheet. He looked helplessly at me.

I heard Victoria moan. "You know Alex is terrified of water, you idiot! Do something!"

"Cast off!" said Grandad. He must have given up with the knot.

"Cast off!" chorused Sophie. "Aye, aye, Captain!"

I took hold of the rope attached to the tree.

"Pull!" I shouted to the others. "Get the boat closer to the bank!"

I felt the weight of the water on the rope, burning skin off my palms.

Lia was pulling now too, and Leonard, but however much we tried, we couldn't seem to bring the boat any nearer. The current was so strong. Too strong.

"Cast off, damn you!" shouted Grandad. He jabbed an oar into the water. The boat leaned horribly to one side, then thumped back down.

Sophie must have started to realize this wasn't a game after all. "I want to get off now," she whimpered. "Want to get off." She walked down the boat, which lurched with every step.

"No!" we all roared together.

The word hung on the air. Sophie stopped where she

was. She stared at us, her mouth opening and closing like a fish, but no words coming out.

She lost her balance.

I saw her surprise change into fear as she started to wobble, slowly at first and then faster and faster, and then her legs gave way under her and she clutched at the air. She gave a little screech and seemed to hover over the rushing water a moment and there were no sounds and there was no movement, nothing. . . She fell backwards.

We all screamed. Sophie's face bobbed to the surface, her hair plastered flat on to her skull. By some miracle she was holding the rope. Both hands. The current made trenches of water around her face and her eyes were huge.

"Hold on, Sophie! Don't let go!" sobbed Victoria, trying to get up, but not able to. "For God's sake, do something, someone!"

I looked at the dark swirls of water. I couldn't seem to pull my eyes away from them. Their smooth hills and dips rising and falling and curving like the sleek backs of snakes. Rising . . . falling. . . Rising . . . falling. . .

. . . Babo had taught me to swim. I'd been the best seven-year-old swimmer in my village. . .

Water splashed over Sophie's mouth. Her head jerked up in panic.

. . . But I hadn't swum since then. Not since that day the men with guns came. . .

I saw Sophie's fingers trying to keep hold of the rope as the snakes of water slithered round her.

. . . I didn't even know if I still knew how.

*You can't go in*, a voice inside me taunted. *You never were a good swimmer. Not good enough. Don't you remember what happened, Alex? Don't you remember what happened to your little brother?*

I stared down at the murky, speeding water. My head was wet with sweat. I couldn't move. I wanted to curl into a ball. I couldn't even do that.

Any minute Sophie would let go. Any minute she'd be swept away.

I couldn't move. I couldn't do anything.

I saw Sophie's head turn in the water, like it was really hard for her to do it, and then she was looking straight at me. I swear. Just at me.

*Help me Alex*, the eyes said. *Upomoć, Alex! Upomoć!*


. . . I squeeze my eyes shut. Feel myself pull off my shoes. I don't let myself think. I look for where the rope skims the water between the bank and Sophie. I feel my fingertips touch. My head bends forward between my arms. . .

I dive in.

The water hits and straightaway the cold knocks the air out of my lungs. I come up, spitting and coughing, snatching at the rope. I get a hold and grip it. It cuts right into the backs of my knuckles. My body is shaking. I want to vomit, but I force myself to go on. Hand over hand I haul myself along the rope.

Water splashes up and over me and I struggle to keep

sight of Sophie. I see her fingers like little hooks on the rope. I see the water prising them off, one by one. I need to go faster, but the current squeezes me. It feels like I am trying to swim through mud.

I grit my teeth and drive myself on. I am close now. I can maybe nearly catch on to her, if only I can get a bit closer. Sophie's left hand comes off the rope and she twangs sideways like a snapped elastic band and her head is right back and the water is all round her face and then I see her last finger is sliding from the rope and there is no more time.

One hand on the rope, I lunge forward. I have her wrist. . . Her hand. I fasten my freezing fingers around hers. But already I feel her slipping. I see her other hand arch towards me, grabbing at nothing. I gasp for air. I squeeze her hand tighter and try to swim. Screaming pains shoot through my arm muscles as I drag us along the rope.

The river zigzags round us, making blades of water curl over our shoulders.

I feel myself slowing down. Sophie is getting heavier and heavier. My jeans are saturated. My legs are made of stone. Sophie's hand goes limp and her eyelids are half closed. I know I can't hold her much longer. . .

I have a desperate, mad idea.

With a cry, I heave Sophie towards me. I hug her as close as I can. She clings tight and twists, making me go under. I hold her. Try to get the belt from my jeans. I have to get it round Sophie. Have to loop it over the rope. . .

. . . The buckle won't open. The metal is too slippery. My fingers are too cold.

I wrench the leather back. Again. Again. The metal spike comes free.

I inch the belt around Sophie. Somehow stop her head from sinking. I fasten the buckle over the rope. It's slipping. No. My arms burn with pain. No! I swat the water from my eyes. . .

The belt loop goes taut and takes the weight. Can the strap cope with the strain? I ease along the rope again, Sophie clamped to me. Water slaps my face. My eyes sting. I try to make out the stretch of blurry, racing river between us and the bank.

Suddenly a big wave hits.

It comes from nowhere. It knocks us apart. I have Sophie by only one hand.

Her fingers are slipping.

I let go.

I let go of her hand.

I can't see her.

The rope she was belted to is underwater. I thrash around for her. I try to shout her name, but my mouth fills up.

Panic suffocates me. It is happening again. It is my fault this time too. I scramble around in the filthy water. I made the scrapbook. I've forced Grandad to remember. Remember things that were best forgotten. This is all my fault.

All around it seems the river is taunting me as it slides past. It hisses and whispers and mocks me. It calls me terrible names. It says Grandad is a fool. Brain-dead. Better off in a grave.

Anger boils up in me. I want to punch the stretched belly of water, pound it into a pulp. Destroy it.

I leap forward through the water with a yell and I hit the water with my fist. I kick at it. I clench my teeth and I clutch the rope and I pull. The cord slices into my fingers and pain shoots up my arms, but I keep pulling. Water pours into my mouth but I spit it out and keep pulling. . .

Sophie breaks the surface.

Her eyes are closed. Her head is tilted back.

I wrestle her close and smack my arms against the current. The roaring water claws me down.

Over the noise of the river, I hear muffled shouts from the bank. My face keeps going under, distorting the sounds. I hear voices too, a snatch of words. . . I don't know if they are real or in my head. . .

*We've got to save them. We've got to bring them home.*

I grip Sophie's hand harder and jolt her through the water with me. The river surges around us, but I keep pulling and pulling.

I haul Sophie through the water. I hurl myself against the current.

I haul and I twist and I fight. . .

. . . Until I know I can't fight any more and I don't have

a single bit of strength left and that's when I start swallowing water. . .

. . . That's when I feel something under my foot, and it must be mud and I am slipping against it, trying to get a hold, and Lia and Leonard are yanking my arms and then I am panting on the bank with the sharp taste of river water in my mouth and I am on my knees and I am checking for a pulse on Sophie's throat but I can't find one and I am pushing up her chin, the way my babo taught me, and I am pinching her nose and blowing air back into her lungs. . .

Only it isn't Sophie's face I see.

It is my little brother's.

It is Nicu.

I thump at his chest.

Sophie's body arches upwards. She coughs and wheezes, water spurting from her mouth. She gives a weak moan.

But Nicu is still not moving. His face looks like a white mask.

Sophie's eyelids flutter open and she blinks.

But Nicu lies there in the mud. Eyes wide. Empty.

Sophie struggles up to sitting, groaning and shivering.

I lie on my back in my soaked clothes, tasting silt in my mouth.

I hold Nicu's hand through the mud. . .


I was aware of Mum and Victoria somewhere nearby in hysterics, and Sophie was wailing and I think I saw Dad gripping her and I think I heard him shout, "This is the last straw!"

I think Lia was nearby saying something to me, but I can't remember what.

I think that Grandad was sitting in the wobbling boat with the oar in his hand, staring at the water.

I lay there, looking up at the tree branches and the swirling storm clouds. I knew it was over. I'd been so close to telling my family the truth. I knew that what had just happened was too bad, too wrong to ever forget about, whatever I told them now. I knew for sure that they'd never let Grandad stay. Not now.

I wiped my hands over my face. My fingers dripped blood down my cheeks, but I hardly noticed.

I closed my eyes and when I opened them again Leonard was stooping over me. He was looking at me in a different way to how he usually did. Something was weird, like he was wearing a disguise or something. Maybe he had taken one off. Anyway, I didn't get it at first, but then I realized what was so strange. He was smiling at me, but not in the usual nasty Leonard way. He was smiling at me and he was crying and he was holding out his hand to help me up.

# 23

# Telling the Truth

*Miss Kirby's house. 6:15 p.m. Strolling down Memory Lane.*

Miss Kirby laid the photographs down on the table and let out a long sigh. She refilled my glass with lemonade and sat in the armchair next to mine with her teacup.

"I'll tell you whatever you want to know, Alex."

It had taken me a while to get out of the house. Mum and Dad hadn't wanted me to go anywhere, but I'd insisted I needed a walk. Finally, when the doctor had been and we'd all had hot baths and Sophie was sleeping, and Mum had hugged me for the three millionth time and said I was their hero, she and Dad had at long last agreed I could go out.

I felt nothing like a hero. That was the last thing I felt. I knew it was over for Grandad. But somehow I wanted to see things through to the end for him. It seemed the right thing to do. Fill the last gaps in his story. Have all the questions answered.

I stared at the bandages across my palms as I held my

glass. It was like having to wear a pair of weird, fingerless gloves. My hands still stung from the rope burns. But there was something a lot worse than that. The tight feeling across my chest. A pain that spiralled through me every time I took a breath.

I gulped my drink and let the fizzy, sweet taste make bubbles in my throat. I tried to focus on what I still wanted to know.

"When he was on the boat, Grandad said something about saving our boys," I said. "Did he mean at Dunkirk?"

Miss Kirby gave a slight nod. "William was beside himself when Tommie died, but he still managed to ferry more than two dozen soldiers from the beaches to the waiting navy ships. That's what he got his medal for. Did he ever tell you about that?"

I shook my head. Grandad's words came back to me. *I don't believe in medals. . . Bits of metal stuck on the chest of a corpse.*

"Well, he gave the medal away, the first chance he got," Miss Kirby continued. "He couldn't stand looking at it, he told me."

She shuddered. "I can't even begin to think what that must have been like, actually being there at Dunkirk, with all the shelling going on around. If people in the village had known what William went through, I'm sure they would have left him alone."

I sipped more lemonade and let her keep talking.

"They were little more than children themselves when

they married, Freda and Tommie. He was twenty, she was nineteen. She was going to have the baby, you see. They'd only been married a few weeks when he died.

"When Freda died, we all had our suspicions who had started the fire, but there was never any proper proof. No real evidence. Just hearsay. It was put down to faulty wiring in the end, actually. But Freda's death. . ." Miss Kirby's eyes had tears in them. ". . . It was almost too much for your grandad to take. It was a terrible shock. For all of us. But he was devastated.

"I found him standing on Doverham cliff once. He was right on the very edge, staring down at the sea crashing on the rocks. It made me so afraid, seeing him standing there like that. But before I could get to him he'd stepped back of his own accord. Do you know what he told me later? He told me that he had to carry on. He had to go on, for your dad."

I thought about that baby. That little boy who saved Grandad's life.

Miss Kirby took the cosy off the teapot and topped up her cup. "Do you know something, Alex? If it hadn't been for your dad, I think your grandad might have gone off the edge that day."

If he had? All the what-ifs whirred round inside my head. No Grandad, no Alex of Doverham. No train sets, no Alzheimer's, no burnt buried pillows, no scrapbook, no saving Sophie. . . The whirring what-ifs became one big blur.

"So William was faced with bringing your dad up alone," said Miss Kirby. "Then Mildred stepped in. It was hard for your grandad to say no. I think he suffered from depression for a long time. Your dad didn't have the easiest of starts, put it that way."

I put down my glass and picked at the threads of a cushion. Dad. Grumpy Dad who always worked too much. I felt guilty. . . Maybe he had to work too much. He had four children, after all, most of them with expensive tastes. Maybe the way he was with Grandad, maybe it wasn't really his fault. He'd only believed too much of what Great-Aunt Mildred had told him. Maybe Dad wanted Grandad in the Sunflower because he was worried something might happen to us and he was trying to protect us. Protect Grandad too. I even felt a bit sorry for bitter and twisted Great-Aunt Mildred.

"Remember this?" Miss Kirby passed me a small, frayed book.

*The Unknown Battle of Dunkirk. Photography by W. G. Smith.*

"Mr Webb thought your grandad's photos were an insult to his brother's memory. He would hassle him every chance he got. I gather he got worse just before he died."

I turned the pages of the book with my fingertips, recognizing more photographs from Dunkirk.

"Your grandad was an easy target for lots of people," said Miss Kirby. "Especially because he was already in their bad books for being a C.O. I suppose getting at him was a kind of outlet for their grief. But when we lose loved ones . . . well, we both know how terrible that feels."

She looked hard at me. "Alex, whatever your grandad forgets, he still loves you very much. Remember that."

She fingered the pile of photographs on the table.

"I wanted to organize an exhibition of your grandad's work at the library, but the authorities wouldn't let me. William even got hounded by some government officials at one point. They said it was bad for public morale to have images like that around."

I sat up. Grandad going on about being watched. People after him.

"Maybe people were right not to like your grandad's photographs," mused Miss Kirby. "Remember, more than half of the young men in our village were wiped out. Maybe your grandad should have waited longer and tried to spare their families' feelings a bit. But he felt it was important to tell the truth, and there never would be a right time for something like that, would there?"

Miss Kirby's eyes glazed over and she stared at the mantelpiece, at a row of framed photos. "We all lost people we loved." She pulled her handkerchief from her sleeve and wiped her eyes. "In my case, William's photographs helped me come to terms with the death of someone I'd lost. I wanted to know the truth, you see. I wanted to see what it was like. What really happened. However painful that was." A few tears ran down her cheeks. "Your grandad's photos helped me to grieve my Robert."

I longed to be able to cry too. Why couldn't I cry? I took a corner of the cushion in my bandaged fist and stared down at a page in the book.

The expression on the soldier's face.

I'd seen that look before.

On the face of my babo.

That day.

My head hurt. The pain in my chest was getting worse. I closed the book and held it out to Miss Kirby.

"Keep it." She rested a hand on mine and then sat back with her tea. "You must add it to your scrapbook."

I nodded. "Thanks." I stood up. "I've everything I need now. Not that there seems much point in the scrapbook any more. . ."

I thought Miss Kirby's cup would smash, the way she slammed it down on to her saucer. Blobs of tea splashed on to the carpet. She leapt up and gripped my arm hard. She took me totally by surprise. She was a lot stronger than she looked.

"There's still plenty of point, Alex," she said. "For you, as well as your grandad."

"Me?" I stared at her.

"That's part of why you did this, isn't it?" she asked. She still had hold of me. "So long as you look at your grandad's past, you don't need to look at your own."

I opened my mouth to say something like, *What are you talking about?* or *Course not* but I couldn't get any words out.

I felt her grip tighten. The muscles in my arm throbbed. "But you'll have to, won't you? Look at your own past? If you're going to collect *all* the parts of your grandad's life . . ."

*Stop.*

". . . that includes the part with you in it too."

*Stop.*

". . . When you first met in the refugee camp."

*No. STOP!* I closed my eyes. Blotted out her voice.

The image came back to me. An image through a red skin of water.

That look on my babo's face

just

before

they

pressed

the

trigger

# 24

# Canute's Sandcastle

*The beach. Saturday morning. Turning back the tide.*

today
was
Grandad's
last

I watched him standing by himself on the edge of the sea while Mum rolled out a big tartan rug. We had the beach to ourselves, just a boy flying a kite in the distance. It was the perfect setting for the final happy family picnic (plus Lia) before Dad drove Grandad to the Home for the Virtually Dead and Buried. Mum had made the announcement about the Sunflower at breakfast, while she'd heaped extra helpings of bacon and fried bread on to our plates. The sun was even out. The sand still had a damp feel, and we had to keep our coats on, but she had been determined.

Sophie was building a castle with her bucket and spade.

Victoria was sitting, scooping out a moat, and Dad and Leonard were reinforcing the towers with pebbles. Mum went over to join in.

I sat on a corner of the rug at Lia's feet watching them, rolling a football from one bandaged hand to the other.

One big happy family.

Lia had something in a small carrier bag. She'd been clutching it ever since her dad dropped her off but she wouldn't tell me what was in it, even though she looked like she was dying to. From the way she was fidgeting around in her seat I could tell she was massively overexcited about whatever it was. Knowing her, she wanted to enjoy a bit of suspense first. As if I didn't have enough of that already.

I had the scrapbook hidden inside my coat. I'd decided that everyone should still know the truth about Grandad's life. I was going to tell them as soon as we sat down to eat. I was scared of how they'd take it. Especially Dad. Most of all Grandad. Really scared. But whatever happened, I knew that it was important for them to know. I'd decided that no family should have that many secrets from each other. Not big secrets like that. It wasn't right.

I carried on watching Victoria and Sophie and Dad and Leonard and Mum, and I thought about families. How a family was like a sandcastle. A fortress. Something that should be safe and amazing and unbreakable, but could crumble to nothing once the first waves hit.

But Miss Kirby had got me thinking. I was going to tell

them, however much my stomach was tying itself in knots right then. I was going to tell them the truth.

Leonard left the others and flopped down on the opposite corner of the rug to me and hacked the sand with a stick.

He glanced up at Lia, and then at me. "I was the one who did it," he said.

I looked at him, trying to work out what he was going on about.

"I messed up Grandad's darkroom," he said. I heard Lia give a little gasp behind me. The stick snapped and he tossed it away. "I wanted you to get blamed for it. I pinched the padlock key while he was asleep."

I watched Grandad's back, silhouetted against the sea. "It doesn't matter," I told him.

Leonard prodded the sand with his foot. "I never would have told, you know. About Grandad burning his pillow.

"I suppose I was . . . well, jealous, of the way you and Grandad got on. I never would have got him into trouble. . . I guess I liked winding you up about it."

"It's OK. Really." I nodded at him. Managed a smile.

Leonard stared out at the waves. "By the river yesterday. . ." He paused. "I didn't have the guts to. . ."

"It doesn't matter," I said.

"It does to me!" He gave a dry laugh. "Don't suppose I could be a soldier after all."

I kicked the ball to him with a flurry of sand. He scrambled up, headed it back, then ran to rejoin the others.

"Alex." From the way Lia was swerving her chair from side to side waggling her carrier bag, I guessed the suspense had got too much for her. She pulled out a box and passed it to me. It was flat and square, about the size of my hand, and covered in some sort of dark blue, fuzzy velvet stuff. "My dad found this," she said breathlessly. "At the last antiques fair, the military memorabilia one."

I stared at it.

"Open it then!" she hissed.

For some reason my heart started to thump.

I ran a fingernail under the lid of the box. Its rusty hinge creaked as I eased it open.

Inside was a medal, on a frayed stripy red and gold ribbon. It was round and there were two swords or daggers crossed at the top and an anchor shape curving around the bottom. There was a fierce-looking lion hovering over water, with an ill-looking dolphin or a whale or something below it.

"The lion, well, that stands for good, apparently, and the dead sea monster in the water, well, that symbolizes evil, so the whole thing is like good winning over evil. . ." Lia seemed about ready to burst. "Look on the other side, won't you!"

I turned the medal over and rested it on a bandaged palm.

There was something on it that looked like Aladdin's lamp with a smoking flame and . . . I stared.

Below the lamp, in capital letters, it said *DUNKERQUE, 1940*.

"Can you believe it?" said Lia. "That's not all. That's not

all! Look at the box again." She looked like she would throttle me if I didn't get a move on. "Look at the box!"

I looked back at the box. In the circular hollow where the medal had been, there was a piece of card stuck to the fabric. There was something written on the card in looping gold letters.

I could hardly take in what I was reading. It was impossible. It couldn't be. Could it?

### *William George Smith, Doverham*

"Well, say something!"

After all this time.

"Alex?"

What were the chances?

"Alex!"

"Grandad's medal," I managed to croak.

"My dad couldn't believe it when he found it. It's pretty amazing it turned up, don't you think? Anyway, my dad says you can have it, obviously. It's just too brilliant. You can show it with the scrapbook."

Her words jolted me back to what I had to do. What I was going to say. Suddenly I felt very nervous, like I had bad stage fright or something. What if I didn't tell the story right or if I missed things out? What if I totally forgot what to say? What if it came out all wrong? What if nobody believed me?

Mum sat down with us and I quickly hid the medal in

my pocket. She dusted sand off her skirt and started unscrewing a flask. "Lunch is ready!" she called, and everyone came and sat down on the rug. Grandad was on a folding chair by the edge.

I felt sick.

"It's now or never," whispered Lia. She put a hand on my shoulder.

Mum started passing round the paper plates. There was French bread, and cubes of cheese and chunks of pineapple on cocktail sticks, and hard-boiled eggs.

My throat felt so dry. I gulped down some water from a pink tumbler and wiped my mouth on the cuff of my coat.

"I've got things to tell you," I said.

They hardly glanced up from their chicken drumsticks.

"I've got things to tell you all!" I repeated more loudly.

They were looking at me now: Victoria holding a plastic fork with a cherry tomato speared on it. Leonard with a handful of crisps. Sophie with her head to one side and a ribbon of ham hanging from her mouth.

Mum mid-sip. Dad buttering his bread.

They stared at me. Nobody moved.

I pulled out Grandad's scrapbook from under my coat. I felt my hands shake.

Dad pointed his plastic knife. "Alex, I thought I told you. . ."

"I'm sorry, Dad, but this is important," I said. "I need you all to listen! Give me a chance to tell you what I found out. You have to know the truth about our grandad."

"Alex," Dad cut in. I heard the edge of anger in his voice. "This isn't the time or place to be. . ."

"Let him speak, will you?"

It was Leonard's voice. He pulled Sophie into his lap. "Go on, Alex," he said. He nodded at me and bit into a crisp. He smiled.

I felt Lia squeeze my shoulder. Grandad gave me a steady look.

Suddenly I wasn't afraid any more. I sat there and told them. I told them everything I knew. About conscientious objection and Dunkirk, about Freda and Tommie, about the fire, about Grandad's war photographs, about grief and the terrible things it did to people.

I didn't leave a single bit out. I told them everything. I showed them stuff from the scrapbook to back up what I was saying. Wedding photographs, the sellotaped picture of Peter Webb and his confession letter, Great-Aunt Mildred and Henry, Tommie in army uniform, a copy of the May 13th newspaper article Lia had done for me, the grave rubbing, pages from Grandma's diary, Grandad's book, photographs of soldiers on Dunkirk beaches. . . Nobody interrupted me. Not a single time. Not once.

When I'd finished telling them, everyone just sat staring at me while Grandad's medal dangled in my bandaged hand. Nobody said anything. The breeze ruffled the pages of the scrapbook. Grandad was gripping the sides of his folding chair and his knuckles had gone pure white.

Victoria still had hold of the tomato on a fork. Mum was

looking at me, her mouth hanging open. Leonard was shaking his head from side to side. Sophie gazed from one face to another, her food forgotten. Dad's knife had made a buttery hole in the tartan rug.

The waves sighed as they spread over the sand. Somewhere overhead a lone seagull shrieked.

I heard another noise. A funny sort of breathing. A stifled sob. I saw that Dad was shaking a bit and he had tears on his face. I'd never seen him cry before. Mum went to put her arms around him and she was crying too.

Grandad got shakily to his feet. It was hard to tell what he was thinking. How he'd taken it. Whether he'd even followed what I'd been saying.

But I guessed he must have done because the first thing he did was to come over to me and rest a hand on my head. I felt him stroke my hair.

I held out the scrapbook and he took it from me.

"I loved Tommie so much," he said quietly, but so everyone could hear.

Grandad turned to Dad. "He made me promise to marry Freda. That part was easy. I already loved her, you see."

I saw Dad nod. I felt like I was watching the two of them in a play. I wondered if Leonard and Victoria and Mum felt that way too. Embarrassed and awkward and sad for them all at the same time, and caring so much about what happened next.

Dad pointed at Grandad's scarred hands. "You got those from trying to save Mum?" he asked. "Mildred said it was an accident with some barbed wire when you were putting up fences once. Why didn't you ever tell me the truth?"

"Why didn't you ever ask?" Grandad stared at the sea a moment, but then he looked back at Dad. "It was hard to talk about, Richard," he said. "I often wished I'd died in that fire too. Or on that filthy beach in France with Tommie."

"It was an accident," said Dad quietly.

Grandad hung his head.

"It was," Dad said, more loudly. "You shouldn't blame yourself." I heard him swallow. His voice was breaking with emotion. "Tommie's death wasn't your fault."

A look passed over Grandad's face. Something so raw and painful and loving that it stopped my breath. "Oh, Richard. . . You don't know. . ." His words were all choked up. "You can't know what it means to me to hear you say that, Richard, son."

Dad stepped forward and Grandad was hugging him. It was weird seeing them there like that, and uncomfortable, and happy too. Mum smiled at me and I saw Victoria smile at Leonard as he cuddled Sophie in his lap. Lia beamed at me. Sophie gave Leonard a kiss, and the fairy cake she'd been licking the top off, and then unwound herself from him and came to sit with me. I felt her little arms tighten around me and her warm, sticky breath against my neck.

Dad wiped his eyes and turned to me. "Yesterday, Alex. What happened with Sophie. You did something unbelievable. Unbelievably brave. There wouldn't be a medal anywhere near good enough for what you did."

He hugged me hard and then rubbed a handkerchief across his face. "I think we've got to admit that most of us have been turning a blind eye to what's been happening with Grandad. Alex has been battling by himself all this time to look after him. . ." He whispered something to Mum and she smiled back at him, nodding hard. "From now on we're all going to help."

"We're going to all start doing our bit!" agreed Mum. "We're a family! From now on we're damn well going to act like one!"

Sophie giggled. Maybe it was the effect of too many fairy cakes. Probably it was the shock of hearing Mum swear in a public place. Anyway, as if on cue, she started these great shuddering giggles.

Victoria took one look at Leonard and they burst into a fit of hysterics too. It was the tension, I suppose.

Dad laughed as well and put an arm around Mum. "We'll shove the Sunflower Care Home where the sun doesn't shine!"

"Where doesn't the sun shine, Daddy?" Sophie tumbled over the sand, squawking. "Where doesn't it shine?"

I felt it. The relief. Like the curtain coming down at the theatre.

I'd kept my promise.

Despite everything. I couldn't believe it. I was numb.

I'd kept my promise.

The relief was like a wave. A warm, strong wave, full in the face, knocking you backwards, making you gasp and scream and laugh and. . .

. . . Except, as I watched them, I somehow still felt like I was detached from them all. As if I were watching people in a family that I cared for, that I felt for, but that I wasn't properly part of.

"Stop your racket!" said Grandad. They were all piling around him, my sisters and my mum and my dad and my brother, hugging him, and he was laughing and looking embarrassed and wiping tears away. "Steady on."

I wanted to cry too.

But I couldn't.

I watched the boy's kite spiral and fall and struggle to rise again.

Mum started packing the picnic things away. "The tide's coming in."

Everyone started helping, Lia leaning forward from her chair.

I climbed the long, zigzagging steps that went up the cliff from the beach. Nobody stopped me. They must have understood I didn't want company right then.

At the top I sat on a concrete pillbox and stared out from the headland.

I remembered sitting there with Grandad. The look he'd given me when he didn't know who I was.

It all became clear to me.

I'd worked it out.

It was so simple, really.

I didn't know who I was.

The clouds moved fast across the sky, making shadows skim the water like boats. Waves swirled and hissed on the rocks far below me. I thought about the hundreds of wrecks on the bottom of the Channel. The smoothly moving surface with all that mangled, rusting metal hidden underneath.

To one side, the bay curved away towards Doverham and five figures moved about on the beach.

Somebody sat down next to me, panting. I knew straightaway who it was.

I felt for the medal in my pocket and handed it to Grandad. He turned it over and over in his palm and didn't say anything for a long time.

"Well I'll be damned," he whispered at last.

We stared out across the water in the direction of France.

Grandad stood up. He had the medal in his hand and he raised his arm and looked at the water and looked to me. I nodded.

"This is for Tommie."

He pulled his arm back and I imagined him throwing the medal and I imagined it flashing in the sunlight and arcing over the water and disappearing with a silent silver splash. . .

. . . But then Grandad closed his hand around the medal

and put it in his pocket.

"I'd like to go back there one day," he said. "To Dunkirk. Stand on that beach again. Remember what happened."

He held my hand. "I thought it was better to keep my past boxed up, Alex. But I was wrong." He held my hand tighter. I felt my sores throb. "It suffocates you if you do that. In the end it eats you alive. I've learnt now it's better to face things. However hard it is. However much it hurts."

I stared down at the beach. Soon the water would come and wash the sand smooth and flat. I imagined the fingers of tide on the walls of Sophie's sandcastle, making it slump and crumble.

Grandad held up his hands towards the sea.

"No good," he said, shaking his head with a small smile. "No ruddy good.

"But maybe that King Canute bloke. . ." He laughed. "Maybe he wasn't so daft after all when he claimed he could stop the tide, d'you think? Maybe in reality he was trying to teach his people a thing or two."

Grandad fingered his beard. The bruise under his eye was almost gone. He looked so unhappy, but there was a determination in his voice too.

"I've been thinking about things, Alex. I've been thinking a lot. I've decided that it would be for the best if . . . I think I should go and live at the Sunflower after all."

I gaped at him. At first I couldn't speak. "But Dad said. . ." I stuttered. "Everyone's going to help. . ."

"I know. I know. But after what happened yesterday. . ."

I couldn't believe what Grandad was saying! After everything we'd been through.

"It's not far away," Grandad went on. "We could still see lots of each other. We'll still be a family."

"No!" I shook my head. "No!" But he took hold of my face between his hands, his two scarred hands. I felt the palms press hard. Fierce and sad and loving.

"I couldn't live with myself if something happened to one of you because of me," he said. "You, Alex. You're the most, the most important. . . If it wasn't for you. . ." Grandad bit his lip. "You saved me, Alex! Do you realize that? The first time we met. . . The first time I felt your little hand in mine. . ."

I remembered a room with cracked walls. A row of beds with bars on the ends like cages. Mum and Dad wandering between the rows. Grandad kneeling to talk to me. He'd got it all wrong! It was Grandad who'd saved me, not the other way round!

The figures on the beach had started making letters in the sand, but far up from the tideline so whatever it was they were writing wouldn't get washed away.

We sat and watched them in silence.

W o e u x

I think they might have been using the point of Mum's umbrella, or sticks or picnic knives or something. They were all writing at the same time. Lia to one side. Even

Victoria was hobbling about.

W o e y u L x

Each letter must have been at least as tall as Dad.

W o ve y u Lex

Emotion shuddered through me.

We Love you ALex

Grandad reached out and touched my shoulder. His shadow stretched like a giant along the edge of the cliff.

"In Bosnia. . ." he said. "God only knows exactly what happened to you there. I only know what they told me at the refugee camp, and what I heard you shout in your sleep.

"But the way I see it is, the water saved you. Got you away from the guns. You had to let your brother go, or you'd have both drowned."

I pressed my fingers to my head. I wished the tide would come into my brain. Wash out all the stuff I didn't want. Take all the bad stuff away. Leave my mind smooth and flat and empty and. . .

I felt my teeth clench. I could hardly speak. "But I promised Nicu I'd keep him safe."

Grandad stared out to sea. "Freda pleaded with me to

take the baby first," he said. "I couldn't manage them both. . . I promised I'd go back for her, but. . ."

He squeezed the shoulder of my coat in his fist.

"But some promises can't be kept, Alex. However much you want to keep them.

"Some promises just can't be kept."

My eyes stung, but still no tears came.

Grandad took the scrapbook from inside his coat and held it against his chest.

"That's one of my most important memories, that is. Finding you in that camp. But what about before that?"

I tried to move away from him, but he had a tight hold on my hand again.

"What about before that? What happened to you before that?"

Then he says my name. The name I haven't heard anyone say in years. The name nobody ever uses.

"Alexandru," he says softly. "Alexandru. Don't you think it's time to open your box?"

# 25

# Pandora's Box

I reach under my bed and pull out the box. It is just where I left it.

It is the box they gave to me when I left the camp. When Grandad, Mum and Dad came to adopt me.

I smooth off the dust.

A single elastic band is the only thing that keeps me from opening it.

It has a lid that lifts off, like the lid of a coffin.

I look inside, at the photographs, the letters, the memories of my other life.

Photos Grandad took when we first met.

The pictures I drew in the camp. Crayon guns and crayon blood.

A wedding photograph.

A cutting from a newspaper. A picture of a boy looking out through the bars of a bed.

A photo of the four of us. My other family. Standing

smiling by our house, before they came to burn it down.

There is an envelope. I ease it open. Unfold a thin piece of paper from inside. It is headed *United Nations*. It is flimsy, like a dried leaf, and on it is a list of the dead.

My family are written on it. I touch their names. Carefully, afraid the words will tear. I run my fingers over the letters spelling them out.

My father. My mother. My brother.

Babo. Mama. Nicu.

And finally I can cry. I feel the tears squeeze themselves from me. I can't stop. My chest heaves. I struggle to breathe. I feel like I am drowning. But I don't want to stop. I cry the tears that have been bottled up inside me for too long. I cry and I cry.

For my babo. My mama. For Nicu. For the other fathers and mothers and grandmothers and grandfathers and sisters and brothers from my village.

I cry for that day, when the men with guns came and took away my other life.

What's your earliest memory?

Mine's with Babo, learning to swim, in the deep, cold river near our village. I'm splashing the water and I'm afraid but I'm laughing too. Laughing out loud because I know I can do it.

Alexandru.

Me.

# The Yugoslav Wars (1991-2001)

Yugoslavia was a country in south-east Europe, made up of six republics — Serbia, Croatia, Montenegro, Slovenia, Bosnia-Herzegovina and Macedonia.

Some of these republics wanted to be independent and a lot of fighting took place, with men, women and children caught up in the violence.

Hundreds of thousands of people died, making these Europe's deadliest conflicts since the Second World War.

# Websites

If you would like more information on some of the things mentioned in *The Memory Cage*, you may find the following websites helpful:

**Children's guide to Alzheimer's disease**
www.alz.org/living_with_alzheimers_your_brain.asp

**A guide to growing up in your adopted family**
www.afteradoption.org.uk

# Acknowledgements

My agent, Anne Dewe, who kept believing in me when the sea was choppy.

Everyone from the Scholastic team, my deepest thanks. Stephanie Charamnac for digging me out of the pile, and Polly Nolan, for turning the tide. Jessica, Alex, Sarah, Toni, Lisa, Alyx.

Margaret and Paul. Aldo, Silvana, John, Matt, Kathryn, Sarah, Denis and Sandra, for being the moat.

My Beeston Library group in Nottingham, and writing friends in Palmerston North, Cambridge and Brisbane, for pearls of wisdom. Flavia, Katrina, Vivi, Tomas and Ajla for feedback and flags.

Caroline, Josie, Sarah and Susie, fellow writers and wondrous friends, for providing buckets and spades when the sand was crumbling.

Anna and Elena, for making me remember to collect fairy jewels on the beach.

And Max. For promises kept.